MW00982099

Choices *and* Consequences

CJ PAXTON

Choices and Consequences
Copyright © 2017 by CJ Paxton

No part of this publication may be reproduced, distributed,
or transmitted in any form or by any means, including
photocopying, recording, or other electronic or mechanical
methods, without the prior written permission of the author,
except in the case of brief quotations embodied in critical
reviews and certain other non-commercial uses permitted by
copyright law.

Tellwell Talent
www.tellwell.ca

ISBN
978-1-77302-827-9 (Hardcover)
978-1-77302-826-2 (Paperback)
978-1-77302-828-6 (eBook)

Dedicated too: the one who taught me unconditional love....

...and the ones who helped along the way.

PART ONE: CHOICES

Chapter One: Crisis

"What do you think you're doing? What are you thinking? Why on Earth are you here? Really?"

"Well..."

"Do you honestly think he can help you? How are you going to explain this mess to him?"

"Well..."

"No. He'll probably just think you're completely insane; then what you gonna do?"

"He might not? He might be able to help?"

"Well maybe you don't need him? Maybe you can handle all this on your own."

"I can't do that."

"You can, you don't need any help with this; or maybe just don't deal with the problem at all? Why not simply put this up on a shelf buried in the back of your mind and forget the whole thing even happened? Yeah? Just ignore the problem and hope it goes away; works all the time."

"Well actually..."

"Just forget, ignore and move on. Sound good?"

"No, this has to get dealt with, I can't just forget, ignore and move on; not an option. A person cannot simply store away their problems and hope they go away; it does not work that way."

"Well if you hadn't been an idiot in the first place you wouldn't be here now; because you never would have gotten into this mess."

The argument continued inside the young Miss. Gabriella Harris' mind. She was trying to figure out what she had gotten herself into; and how to change her path, or if she even wanted to change it. Gabriella had so many chances to choose a different path, maybe even a better one, but she chose the one with the most twists and turns. 'One day,' she thought, 'one day you'll get this right, one day you'll stop screwing up everything in your life.' Gabriella could not help but get annoyed with herself; anyone could tell she was carrying on a heated conversation in her head. To see her, one would believe her insane.

The waiting room Gabriella sat in was very small, narrow and plain, with bleak grey walls and old cracked tiles made the floor. One side of the room stood two wooden chairs and a small side table that matched followed by three more wooden chairs leading to the outside door. The side Gabriella sat on was identical except the door on her side lead to an office. The wall across Gabriella had three photographs all evenly spaced out much like the rest of the room.

While arguing with herself Gabriella took a moment to examine the three photographs. The first that hung on the left side was mountain scenery; she could see the snow on top, blue skies and a small stream running between the two mountains, it was beautiful, peaceful.

The second photo hanging dead centre was a waterfall, falling into a deep pool of water with the river flowing from it. In the heart of the waterfall there was the face of a man. The face was very light, faint and could hardly be seen. Gabriella had to tilt her head slightly to see him better. The photo puzzled her; she was trying to understand why there was a face hidden in the waterfall.

The third photo was of the river, fast rushing water, never stopping, never ending, rocks surrounding the rushing water with the trees blowing in the wind.

Gabriella liked all three photos yet she found the centre one more interesting than the other two. The strange face in the waterfall intrigued her; the face constantly staring directly out. It reminded her of one of those paintings that seemed like their eyes are constantly following your every move. Gabriella decided to get a closer look; rising from the hard wooden chair she had been perched on, she crossed the small awaiting room and stood putting her knee on one of the chairs directly in front of the photo examining it while trying to forget her own problems.

Gabriella was nervous; she had never really done this before and unsure if she wanted to go through with it. She'd tried in the past once or twice, she would meet the therapist, sit down with them for two or three minutes saying nothing then walk out not looking back. Gabriella found it unnatural, talking to a complete stranger about ones problems, paying someone to listen; it felt wrong but Gabriella knew she had to; she was out of options. Gabriella's life was completely upside down and she was only falling farther and farther down into that deep dark hole she dug herself, and if she was not careful, she might never get out of it. This had to get dealt with, everything needed to get sorted out before it completely consumed her; Gabriella needed this to be finished; no more running and hiding, it was time to come and face the music.

Gabriella focused more and more on the photograph, she had hoped that by putting all her energy into the photo she just might forget her troubles; even if only for a moment; everything would be all right.

Gabriella tried to see the man in the waterfall, she kept shifting to find his face better, and Gabriela found it oddly comforting and soothing, almost putting her at ease with her troubled soul in some inexplicable way. She dug deeper in her thoughts before finally giving up the argument she was clearly losing with herself, letting her mind get lost in the photograph.

The door to Gabriella's side opened so quietly that she never even heard it. She was so involved with the photo that she had completely forgotten where she was and why. The man Gabriella was waiting for stood quietly in front of his office door, arms across his chest with a smile on his face. He stood there watching her enthralled by the photograph.

He saw this young women under twenty, about five feet tall, slightly large but fitting for her height. Fair yet pretty at the same time, just a simple girl. He could see light scars on the left side of her face just below her cheek going down her neck; this made him very curious. Her medium auburn hair that fell in waves, just touched her shoulders and wide hazel eyes that looked as though she had seen a lifetime of pain yet at the same time there was something so peaceful about them; soft and loving. He could see that she had had a lot of pain and horrors in her past and that she was very troubled and yet there was just something about her; something he could not figure out. The man watching Gabriella had always found enjoyment in watching his new patients before actually talking to them, he could learn a lot just from watching. He liked to see which photograph they were drawn towards; it gave him an idea of the type of person they were and what type of help they were seeking.

Over the years he had noticed that more than half of his patients would chose the third photo, some the first however he found that very few would actually chose the second.

Each photograph had a different meaning. The first, the mountains, told him that for the most part they were at peace with themselves and could find joy in the little things; they usually only needed a bit of guidance with a problem they could not solve themselves.

The second, the waterfall, told him that they were missing something huge in their life; they would have an emptiness, a pain in them and never know or understand why.

The third, the river, told him that they were normally overwhelmed and had trouble slowing down the things in their life. They purely needed someone to help them slow down and gain order in their life.

He always liked it when he got a patient who would choose the second photograph; he noticed that those patients in particular had a greater story to tell. He decided to wait a second longer before making his presents known. He very gently cleared his throat just loud enough that he could not be misheard.

Gabriella jumped at the sound of him; she had not been expecting to be startled. She turned to the man she had been waiting for and stared at him; he was not what Gabriella had imagined.

He was about five feet ten inches, with a slight potbelly, handsome, firm figure for his age. She decided him to be in his early to mid-fifties, short dark brownish-black hair with just a tint of grey on both sides. He had the brightest sapphire eyes Gabriella had ever seen along with a wide inviting 'trust me' smile. He wore jeans and a blue button down shirt that brought out his eyes even more. Gabriella quite liked his appearance and found her self-relaxing slightly from his warm appeal.

'One less thing to worry about,' she thought to herself; now she only hoped his personality and mannerisms were just as appealing.

He did not say anything; he merely turned and walked into his office leaving Gabriella to follow. Gabriella slowly followed him into his office; she stood in the doorway peering into the room. The man had already taken a seat in a large beige padded chair, across from the chair stood a large old couch matching in colour.

Gabriella looked around as she slowly headed toward the couch; he had high bookshelves overflowing with books. She could not make out any with just a glance. She also noticed a small area in the corner for coffee and tea; he had more photographs and a couple of paintings similar to the ones in his waiting room hanging on his lightly blue coloured walls. His office was much more cheerful and light than his waiting room.

Just before taking a seat Gabriella noticed a cross hanging above his desk. It was a beautiful Celtic cross; however, it raised some curious questions in Gabriella's mind about what kind of man she was meeting with.

Once Gabriella finally sat down on his old cushy couch the two of them just sat quietly and stared at each other, after a few small moments the man finally spoke.

"So I take it you are Miss. Gabriella Harris?" he said then sat waiting for her reply but all he received was a confirming head nod. "Well it's nice to meet you, to put a face to the voice as it were."

He was smiling as he spoke to her hoping to get anything out of her.

"Um, as you've probably guessed I'm Dr. Robert Wiseman, you may call me Robert if you'd like."

He continued to smile at Gabriella hoping she would relax a bit more and finally say something but she continued to remain silent and stare into his bright sapphire eyes.

Gabriella was trying to figure out the man across from her to make sure he was the right person to tell her story to; she had not told a soul yet and she believed that it could not be told to just anyone; she trusted she would know the right person when the time came. Gabriella had already gone to three other therapists but each time she waited, she would get this feeling in the pit of her stomach that would make her walk away. Dr. Wiseman continued to sit and wait for Gabriella to say something, anything.

Gabriella was beginning to confuse Dr. Wiseman; in all his years of being a therapist he had never had someone come in and not talk, he wondered if she was simply collecting her thoughts or if she was truly afraid of talking to someone, which made him worry what kind of story this girl had to tell. Gabriella took a deep breath then spoke to him.

"You can call me Gabs... that's what everyone calls me." Gabriella paused for a second then.

"I'm sorry I... I'm trying to make sure of something," she paused again. "I'm sure you can understand, a person cannot just go around and talk to anyone." Gabriella watched Dr. Wiseman's facial expression go from concerning to impressed as she continued.

"When I meet someone new I can normally figure out what type of person they are, let's call it intuition, if I get a bad feeling about someone, I bolt for the door and don't look back. Make sense?"

Gabriella took her eyes off Dr. Wiseman and looked down to the grey carpet covering his floor.

"You feel safe," Gabriella's voice was soft and quiet as she said it, looking back up to Dr. Wiseman; she gave him a soft smile while pulling her arms across her chest. Believing that would protect her, and hoped he had not heard her last statement.

Dr. Wiseman did not remark on Gabriella's statement, he was even more impressed with the young woman before him now. He nodded as he started to respond to Gabriella's first statement.

"You're a very cautious person; I can understand that and respect it. I've been informed about the other three therapists you have seen and they all say the same thing. You come in, sit down, wait a minute or two then walk out. I'd like you to know, you're more than welcome to leave at any time but to be honest I don't think you will; you look like a person who truly needs to talk and I think that if you let me, I can help you." Dr. Wiseman could see the relief in Gabriella's eyes as he spoke.

"Do you mind if I ask you something that might seem a bit personal?" Dr. Wiseman nodded his head allowing Gabriella to continue.

"Are you one of those religious type of person who pretends to understand and show them compassion for someone only to smite them for any wrong doings in their life? Or are you the other kind who accepts that even though somebody's made some terrible mistakes in their life, you still listen and try to help while leaving your personal thoughts and feelings out of the situation?"

Gabriella needed to take a breath before carrying on. "Because here's the thing, if you're the first type, the 'fake' type then I'm going to leave and not waste anymore of our time, but if by chance that you're the other type, and I'm pretty sure you are then I think that ... that maybe you can help me. Now I realize just how blunt and most likely offensive that was ... but I really need to know and there's really no agreeable way to ask such a thing." As Dr. Wiseman took in everything, she saw this huge sigh of relief lift from Gabriella.

Dr. Wiseman was not only shocked but puzzled by Gabriella's question, she was quite an impressive girl and he was trying to figure out how she concluded that he was 'religious' at all; and how she was able to sum up into two categories for how 'religious' people behave. Dr. Wiseman could tell Gabriella was a highly intuitive person, he did not realize just how intuitive she seemed to be. He needed to respond correctly as not to scare her away; he needed to be careful; before agreeing to answer her, he felt the need to ask a few questions of his own.

"Okay, now before I answer you, tell me what makes you think I'm religious? What makes you believe religious people are those two types and why does it matter whether I am religious or what type at all?" Dr. Wiseman crossed his arms and sat further back into his chair feeling slightly smug and pleased with himself for being clever.

Gabriella was impressed that Dr. Wiseman was wise enough to question her; she was convinced that he was going to take everything she had to say very seriously, which was exactly what she needed.

"Well," she started, "the cross above your desk, most people would have a clock there, especially when you sit there, you have a perfect view. The fact that it's Celtic is highly specific; now I can only assume it's from your childhood, so I take it you were raised in the church or at least one of your parents." Gabriella took a breath then continued. "There's also the photograph in your waiting room, the one I was looking at, it has a hidden face in the waterfall. It is supposed to be an image of God, right? Then there's you in particular, you just seem the type all at ease and steady; very together and people like that normally get that way after learning or dealing with some issue or problem; lots do this through finding or re-finding God... Why I believe religious people are either hypocrites or decent is because of the house I grew up in and it doesn't actually matter if you're religious or not Dr. Wiseman I simply don't like dealing with liars and hypocrites."

Gabriella smiled as she took a breath. Once again, Dr. Wiseman was impressed by how intuitive Gabriella seemed to be; how quickly she was able to accurately sum him up; and he was curious to hear about the house she grew up in. He smiled back to her as he responded.

"Hum okay... well you've certainly peaked my curiosity. I am religious but I like to call it Christianity. I was raised Catholic but walked away for a while and when I found my way back to God, the catholic faith didn't seem fitting anymore; that's when I became a born again Christian and that cross belonged to my mother. However, to your question I try very hard not to judge people no matter what they have done. It said *'Do not judge or you too will be judged. For in the same way you judge others, you will be judged, and measure you use it will be measured to you.'* Matthew 7 I believe, if I'm correct; now that being said I am human which means I'm not perfect; however no matter how badly you believe your actions to be I will gladly listen and try to guide you in the best direction, see if I can't help you in anyway, and help bring you to a solution." Dr. Wiseman took a breath now. "Gabriella I will do my best to keep all judgment if I have any at all to myself. Anything you say to me, here in this room is safe; and know that I will not betray your confidence."

Gabriella could do nothing but sit there, her mouth slightly open in complete awe of what she had just heard. The man had quoted the Bible, never in her life had that ever happened before; she could hardly believe that he could have simply pulled a Bible verse out of thin air like it was nothing.

Dr. Wiseman could see Gabriella trying to comprehend what he told her and took the opportunity to ask another question.

"Do you believe in God, Gabriella?"

Dr. Wiseman was curious to know, and his question brought Gabriella's focus back.

"No, I don't actually. I've read books where God or a religion was referenced over the years but ah no, I don't believe in God. Never saw the point." Gabriella gave a slight smile then dropped her eyes once more to the grey carpet under her feet.

Dr. Wiseman simply nodded his head he was a bit surprised by her answer, how she could come to such conclusions of him, his photograph and people in general with knowing next to nothing of God. He was compelled to ask more but before he could Gabriella without taking her eyes off the floor said, "Had a feeling." As if, she was reading his mind.

Dr. Wiseman was completely amazed by the young woman before him; *'what a gift,'* he thought, *'show her, teach her, lead her to me, I am waiting.'* The thought had brought shivered down Dr. Wiseman's spine as it passed his mind, *'Yes,'* he thought, *'Yes I can save her, bring her to God.'*

He was full of joy, excited for his task. Dr. Wiseman would not wait to start, however as much as he was excited to help her he had a great amount of fear for Gabriella. *'Just how close is she to being lost forever? How deep were the devils claws in her back? It might be a hard task to do? Perhaps one truly worth doing though?'* the thought kept spinning around in the good doctor's mind.

"So Gabriella," he began the conversation again getting them back on track. "Would you like to tell me your story now?" Dr. Wiseman was smiling on the inside, excited yet fearful at the same time, eager to hear her story. *'It can't be as bad as she thinks, can it?'* he thought, greatly hoping it was not. Gabriella took one last long gaze at Dr. Wiseman, took a deep breath and nodded her head. She was finally ready to tell her story.

Chapter Two: Beginnings

"I was about ten years old, that's when my life changed. I lived with my parents; my mum was great, she used to tell me stories and sing to me all the time. She was big with the church thing; made me go every Sunday. Everyone loved her, and she was beautiful. She had a similar build to me, same hazel coloured eyes like me, smooth soft skin and wavy auburn hair. Everyone always said I looked just like her. My father was the complete opposite from my mum; I never did understand why they were together. My father had no values, he came to church with us and had people believe he was this great understanding Christian; at home he was a drunk and abusive to my mum. He was this skinny light weight who drank and smoked way too much. Short dirty blond hair and deep blue eyes that looked grey when he drank.

I had just come home from school one day and when I walked in the door I... I walked into the house dropping my bag, I... I saw my mother lying on the couch; I figured she had just fallen asleep so I went to shake her awake when I noticed it. The blood... her blood, was everywhere, I had stepped in it on my way to her... she had cut her wrists. Standing just at the edge of the couch I saw the kitchen knife on the floor, it had fallen out of her hands. She looked peaceful, her eyes close, one would think she was sleep if not for all the blood. I was frozen solid, standing in front of my mother. I don't know exactly how long I stood there for; the next thing I knew my father walked in took one look at my mother then walked away. He didn't say a word, he didn't cry, he looked completely indifferent as if he truly didn't care. I followed my father into the kitchen, watched him call the police then grab a beer out of the fridge, sit down at the kitchen table and start drinking. I glanced back into the living room at my mother then back to my father. I eventually sat down at the table across from my father and waited for the paramedics to come; tears never stopped falling down my cheeks, but I never made a sound. I knew that would irritate my father so I stayed quiet, but I never wiped away my tears.

It took the police and paramedics about twenty minutes to show up. I watched the paramedics collect my mother's body as the police sat in the kitchen with my father asking him questions. It was clear to everyone that my mother took her own life; no one knew why though. My mother was the happiest person I knew.

The police has summed up my father within ten minutes of talking to him; my father was drunk by the time the police arrived and the entire time he was talking to them he kept swearing to his wife for leaving him with me. He kept going on about how it was her job to raise me, not his. When the police were finished with my father, they came to me asking if I would be all right, if I had someone who could come over and look after me. Not trusting my father capable of the job, I told them I would be fine, that I would call my friends' mum. They seemed all right with that and left. I never did call anyone; I didn't have any friends, I had my mother so I had never needed anyone else. I had no idea what I was going to do, what was going to happen or how my father would deal with any of this."

Dr. Wiseman sat still and silent trying to take everything Gabriella was telling him in not wanting to miss a single detail as his heart broke for the ten-year-old little girl in her story. Not realizing that was just the start of her torment.

"My father..." Gabriella continued. "My father... well in my opinion is the scum of the earth. He was always drunk, an abusive man but it only got worse after my mother's death. I'm not fully convinced that he ever actually loved my mother, he certainly never loved me. I had no idea why or how he ever ended up with her. She was light and sweet where he's sour and bitter. I had always believed that he drove my mother to her death. The man's a schmuck, crud and disrespectful and like I said he only got worse; and he scared me. The older I got the more I became afraid of him. So this is how I grew up, I learnt to take care of myself and keep the house in order. I no longer had my mother and I barely had a father, I had no friends, no one around to help guide me so I figured everything out on my own."

"So that was my life for the next five years, fending for myself; the only thing that really changed was my father bringing girl after girl into the house; he played the widower card a lot. I did notice that after a while they all resembled my mother in some way; mostly in appearance; I also noticed that as my father grew older the women were getting younger. Talk about a bad cliché. My father hardly ever said two words to me and I avoided him as much as possible, most days though he could not even look at me. I did not leave the house much, well my room really; except for school and to feed my father. So I had no friends and a father who could not stand the sight of me; I could not see how my life could get any worse; then it did.

It was just after my fifteenth birthday, my father... well my father was drunk and when he was drunk, he would say how much I looked like my mother, and how much he hated it. He couldn't look at me because I reminded him so much of her, the wife that decided it was better to die then have a life with him. It was the only proof I had of him actually loving her in some small way. So one night while I was sleeping my father came up, drunk with his half-empty bottle of beer; he smashed it over my head, and then used one of the broken pieces to slash my throat. I tried to defend myself the best I could but..."

Gabriella leaned slightly forward off the couch rolling up her sleeves to show Dr. Wiseman the scars on her arms and neck; he could already see the scars on her face.

"That's how I got them," looking at her scars herself with a sigh then pushing her sleeves back down to cover her past again. "I always wear long sleeves now, to hide what I can; but I wouldn't even have them if I hadn't... fighting off my own father all because he couldn't stand the sight of me."

Gabriella paused, took a deep breath; talking about her father was more difficult than she thought it would be and she required a quick second. Telling that part of her story was reminding her of every drunken night she had to endure; but that night was the worst by far, she honestly believed she was going to die.

Dr. Wiseman could see tears forming in Gabriella's hazel eyes; he couldn't help but feel deeply for her, to have to experience all those horrors alone, to be treated so cruelly by her own father. He never was able to understand how some parents could treat their children in such a way.

"Are you alright, Gabriella?"

"Oh yeah... sorry just... it's the first time saying it all out loud so..." Gabriella quickly wiped away the tears that were forming before they could fall. "I told you all that because... I thought maybe... it would help you maybe understand me a bit... to understand where I come from sort to speak, perhaps to help explain my current actions."

Gabriella gave a slight laugh to herself while shrugging her shoulders. "Isn't that the way it works? Someone screws up and then they blame their parents? You know the traumatized child grows up into a crazy person or something like that."

Gabriella chuckled at her own though again.

"Or maybe it has nothing to do with what's happening now, just a huge coincidence? I might not be able to tell the difference anymore." Gabriella fell silent again; she kept losing track of her thoughts. Dr. Wiseman just sat back and allowed her to find her place, but after a short moment, he interrupted her thoughts with a question.

"What happened to your father after he attacked you?"

Gabriella pulled her focus back and continued with her story.

"After my father's attack on me, he was arrested and brought up on attempted murder charges. In the end, he was found to be mentally insane, I think it was schizophrenia they said he had, anyway he was sent to the Ridgefield Mental Institution in hopes they could help him. So that's where he is, I haven't seen him since the incident. I was informed that after a year, he broke out and tried to find me but they caught him not too long after his escape.

So I'm fifteen at this point, no mother, and a schizophrenic father, and to my knowledge no other family; I had no clue what I was going to do. The courts were able to find an aunt that I had after a few weeks of digging so I was placed in her and her husband's custody.

Enid and John Montgomery. Enid is my father's sister and John is her husband. I had never met these people, had no idea who they were what kind of people they were and I was being shipped off to live with them. I quickly came to understand my aunt and uncle.

My Aunt Enid, well she's this pretty little house wife. She shares many similarities in her appearance with her brothers. She's early forties, slim figure with dark blond hair and blue eyes; she always wears a long plain skirt with a blouse and flat black shoes. Aunt Enid always drives me crazy, more so when I first came to live with them but every so often, she still gets me going. She's just this little woman who craves the gossip of the town. It's her personality that drives me up the wall, always talking, always needing to be in other people's business. After a week living with her I honestly thought she should join my father down at Ridgefield and leave Uncle John and me on our own.

My Uncle John... well, we get along quite well actually. He's a quiet, simple sort of man; the complete opposite to his wife. I like him. He's tall and lanky, around fifty-two and always looks exhausted. I figured that was due to Aunt Enid never shutting up. Uncle John used to be a navy man before retiring, very hard worker but at home, he doesn't do much. At first, I thought he was very boring but he grew on me. The thing I like the most about Uncle John is his ability to tune out whatever he doesn't want to listen to. I envy him for that.

So anyways, that's how I ended up here in Babylon. Moving here was the first time ever being in a small town; it took me a bit to get used to living here; I found everything a little too quiet for what I was used to. The sound of cars and the busy outside world used to put me to sleep, but Babylon was too silent for me at first. I quite like the quiet now. Anyways, I was just glad I didn't have any friends at the time. I didn't mind picking up everything and moving because there was really nothing left where I was and I was excited to start new.

Wanting to start over, however, did not make me any better at meeting people though. I showed up at the beginning of the summer and Aunt Enid decided to take me everywhere with her. I hated all her friends, all annoying and talked way too much; all at the same time too. I always sat to the side keeping to myself for the most part. Lucky for me though, another kid that got dragged around by his mother. This is how I met David Thompson. His mother who I found out was actually his adopted mother; did not like the fact that David didn't like to do anything but read mechanic magazines so she would drag him out of the house with her.

David's a good guy, same age as me. He's this scrawny guy who if he tried could bulk up and get some muscles. When we first met it didn't take me long to understand why he had little to no friends, on top of being kind of small, he's also slightly paler than everyone else; made him an easy target for bullies. Nevertheless, he's an absolute sweetheart. We became friends pretty much because we ended up spending almost every day of the summer together. His mother and my aunt kept pushing us together. I ended up liking David and once he got more comfortable hanging out with me I could tell he liked having me as a friend too. Once David had a friend though, he wouldn't stop talking and asking questions. It was as if he had never talked to anyone in years and he was trying to make up for lost time. He told me he was an orphan, doesn't remember his birth parents, they died but he was never told how or why; anyway he got adopted when he was four. His parents are nice, you never see them fight, non-drinkers and fully active in their church. They used to invite me but I never felt comfortable going, even though my aunt continually tried to make me. David has this theory about God and that he believes in him but if God wanted him, he would know where to find him; so when David turned thirteen he stopped going to church with his parents.

David is a curious type of guy; after he told me everything about himself, he started to ask questions that were all about me; about my past, my scars. I never did tell him; I still haven't. I didn't want people to know so every time he brought up the subject of me I quickly changed the topic to a type of car or what new mechanic book he got and he'd soon forget he had asked me anything at all.

David became my first friend since my mother and it was nice to have someone again. With David, I finally started to feel like a normal kid again. I had people who cared and worried about me; for the first time in years I was able to have a normal summer; I even got to have a birthday that didn't entail hiding away; I got to celebrate turning sixteen with someone I could call a friend. Near the end of the summer, Aunt Enid told me she had enrolled me in Babylon High and that she had already gotten everything I needed. David was happy, he'd have a friend going in and I was glad I would know at least one person.

Babylon High is where I came into my current predicament. My three years of confusion and conflict." Gabriella paused there for a second to gather her thoughts again.

"Just so you know Dr. Wiseman I'm in my final few weeks of school." Dr. Wiseman nodded but stayed quiet; he wanted her to continue with her story. Gabriella was quickly trying to organize her thoughts; she had a lot to tell Dr. Wiseman and didn't want to leave anything out.

Dr. Wiseman decided to take advantage of Gabriella's pause.

"High school, that's where your situation arose?" he didn't say it so much as question but more of a statement. Gabriella simply nodded and continued with her story.

"I found that there wasn't anything really different between Babylon High and other schools I've attended. There were still cliques and popular kids, unpopular, cool trends and un-cool. Babylon High has all the same types of clubs any other school has. Going to Babylon I had simply hoped I would be invisible like I was in my previous schools. David wasn't popular so I hoped that would make things easier; if I hung out with an unpopular student, I thought it would make me the same as him.

First year of high school would be considered a horrifying experience for most people; for me I really couldn't categorize it as horrifying. I saw high school as one-step closer to my freedom; the freedom to no longer need a guardian and I could go back to taking care of myself.

As David predicted we ended up in all the same classes. I remember my first day; everyone kept staring at me as if they knew what my life had been. Course they were really staring because I was the new girl. David found it exciting everyone curious about me; I found it annoying, so much for being invisible.

The day went by smoothly at first, math, science, gym then after lunch David and I had history followed by English. I had no problems with my day until we reached English. I always like to sit at the very back of the class, easier to hide but unfortunately, there was no back. The farthest I could go was right in front of the teachers' desk, which took up a considerable amount of the back and the rest was full of bookshelves and art projects, models. The two seats in front of the teachers desk were free cause everyone else had avoided them, so because David and I got lost trying to find the class they were the only seats left.

Even though the bell had rung and we were all in our seats waiting, our teacher was nowhere to be seen so we all actually had to sit and wait for him to show up. When he finally walked in, I could hardly believe my eyes; I recognized him, yet I knew I'd never met him before; it drove me insane trying to figure out why I recognized him.

In walked this 6" lean, well-built handsome man who could not have looked to be about thirty-six, thirty-seven years old. With his chiseled appearance, smooth creamy skin, deep dark honey eyes and his unshaved stubble look surrounding his well-formed lips; beautiful dark luxurious ash brown hair. He wore a very casual attire; denim dark blue jeans, with a white button-down shirt with his top three buttons undone, and a grey blazer over top. He had every female student's undying attention when he walked in; one look from him and you'd melt in your seat from his inviting 'trust me' smile. He had this awe about him, this mysterious appeal; you could tell he was an old soul and that he had a story you'd want to know yet at the same time you weren't so sure. Then I recognized him; he was the man from the photo.

Every night when my mother would tuck me in, she would always tell me a story about when she was younger. She really liked telling me about her high school days; she was popular so her experience was good. She'd tell me about all the fun she had, the parties, the trouble and drama her and her friends would get into, what her girlfriends were like back then. Anyway, she had this one friend; my new English teacher, from her stories and how she talked about him; they seemed to be like David and I. They met because their science teacher made them lab partners; he was the new kid, unpopular but my mother never abode by the rules of cliques so they became friends and she made everyone else except him into their group. They shortly realized they had most classes together which was good for my mother cause he would always help her out when she needed it; which was most of the time; she wasn't unintelligent just not quite as smart as him. She used to joke that you'd never see one of them without the other; mum told me he was one of the most loyal friends she ever had. I loved hearing her stories, about her school days, summer vacations; she had this gift for making everything sound like some great adventure. I used to ask her about her friend, I was curious to know what had happened to him? Where he ended up? The most she would tell me is that they went to college together but drifted apart and had no idea where he was or what he was up to. I guess I figured out where he ended up, teaching high school English."

Dr. Wiseman found the need to stop Gabriella for a moment.

"So your mother's high school friend ended up being your English teacher?" he looked concerned; while Gabriella sat with a small smile on her face understanding his concern.

"Oh yeah, it gets better though." She replied. Dr. Wiseman nodded his head and allowed her to continue, curious on how it could get better.

"So the teacher's late, he starts off by apologizing then introduced himself.

"Right my name is Mr. Knox and well this is English ten which of course you all already know. So let's just go over a few things and then get started shall we." He glanced around the room casually as he spoke with his beautiful Scottish accent. Not really looking at anyone in particular, he was too distracted trying to organize the mess of papers he was carrying. Mr. Knox continued to speak about everything the class was going to cover over the semester, and then started to do attendance. It was alphabetical so I tuned out until he reached my name. David nudged me so I looked up to Mr. Knox; he had finally looked up from all his papers and was peering around the room as he called out my name. He seemed to be searching for the face that went with the name; when I made myself known to him, his dark honey shaded eyes set on me and his look was unforgettable. It looked as though he was staring at a ghost. I got the feeling he was seeing my mother through me; everyone had always said just how much I looked like her. Mr. Knox's eyes never left mine and I knew he thought I was my mother; our eyes alone were almost identical. He seemed to be in shock and apparently paralyzed; so surprised to see me sitting before him. The class began to whisper amongst themselves as Mr. Knox continued to stare at me. I could hear everyone's whispers going around the room but my eyes never left his. "Does he know her? Why is he just staring at her? Standing there like an oaf? She's not that pretty. Who is she? What makes her so important?" and so on. Even David leaned into me asking if I knew what was happening. I shook my head no, for some reason I didn't want David to know why Mr. Knox was staring. Mr. Knox finally composed himself and continued with attendance dropping his gaze back to his stack of papers so I was out of his line of vision. Mr. Knox and I avoided eye contact for the majority of the class and when the bell rang, I grabbed my things and left as fast as I could. Poor David was so confused by the whole ordeal but I figured I'd explain everything later, later when I knew more."

Gabriella stopped to see if Dr. Wiseman wanted her to continue and to see how much time was left. He told her they had a little more time and to please continue.

Chapter Three: Confusion

"I wasted no time getting home that day from school, ran into the house and straight up to my room; threw my bag to the side and headed straight for my bookshelf. I grabbed my mother's photo album, sat down on my bed, and started flipping through looking for pictures of Mr. Knox. He was in almost every picture with my mother; I always had the feeling from her stories that they were more than friends, but I never did get the proof. I could hardly sleep that night, my mother's stories of Mr. Knox and my imagination kept me up that night wondering of all the possibilities, curious of how he ended up an English teacher. My mother's stories had shown him to be heading into politics, not someone who would enjoy spending their days locked up in a classroom. That was the only part of their story I didn't know.

The next day David kept asking me about what happened in English. I could hear the buzz around the school; most of the students were talking about it. I didn't tell David that Mr. Knox was an old friend of my mothers, I hardly knew what happened in class so I was not about to say something and have it all wrong. I told David that maybe I simply reminded Mr. Knox of someone, which wasn't a complete lie and for all I knew that's what really happened, I couldn't know what was going through his mind; I never talked to him, how could I know what was really going on. I hoped I only reminded him of someone from his past and that he simply couldn't put his finger on who.

I was not that lucky.

"My morning was weird, I had mostly the same classmates in all my classes and apparently no one had anything better to talk about than what had happened the day before in English. Everyone stared at me while they talked, coming up with ideas about Mr. Knox and myself. I found it really quite annoying; second day of school and I already had rumors going around about me; I really am like my mother. English was after lunch so when David and I headed for it I was not looking forward to an hour of more whispers. To my surprised, the class went all right; no one wanted to talk about yesterday in front of the teacher; and Mr. Knox barely looked at me, he scarcely looked at anyone. I thought that maybe I had gotten off the hook, that the whole thing was just a freak accident and didn't mean a thing. That I had gotten lucky this time but just before the end of class, as Mr. Knox walked past my desk to his he dropped a small envelope on my book while making sure no one had seen before taking his seat. I stared at the envelope in horror trying to figure out why and what it could possibly hold. The bell rang and David and I gathered our books and headed out, I quickly tucked Mr. Knox's envelope into my book out of sight from everyone, even me. I wasn't sure what to do with it; I gathered it was a letter but questions kept swarming in my mind. *'What could it say?' 'What could he want?' 'Do I really want to know what it says at all?'* The thought of his letter consumed me for the rest of the day as I tried to figure out what to do with it. David could tell I had something on my mind, something distracting me; he was still asking me about the day before and I still didn't know what to tell him. Tell David, I hardly knew what to tell myself. Secret letter? I had no idea what was going on and until I did, I was keeping David out of it. All I knew was that my mother's old friend? Lover? Someone? Our teacher was dropping me a mysterious letter on my desk when no one was looking. How could I explain that to David? I couldn't even explain it to myself. I decided to wait and not risk it.

"When I got home Mr. Knox's letter was burning a hole in my pocket. I still wasn't sure I wanted to read it but as usual, my curiosity was getting the best of me. I ran into the house, up the stairs ignoring my Aunt's voice and went right to my room locking the door behind me; I didn't want anyone to interrupt me. In my room I have this secret little spot where I can hid away when my aunt is looking for me; it's just above my bedroom ceiling. It is part of the attic that got sealed off from the rest so I turned it into my own little haven. It's small and tight; I covered the floor in large multi-coloured pillows and blankets while the walls were covered with pages of poems, articles, art, anything I found interesting. Just off to the side it has a two shelved bookcase overflowing with my very favorites. Dickens, Shakespeare, Edger Allen Poe, Austen, Bukowski, Keats; etc. I had always enjoyed the latter period. I feel safe there; it's the only place in the house that makes me feel at home. So I climbed up, pulled out Mr. Knox's envelope from my bag, opened it and pulled out a short letter. I settled down in my nook and read:

Miss. Harris,

I realize that this is all very unorthodox; however, I could not contain myself in writing you. I believe my eyes are playing tricks on me and I am hoping you can clarify a few things for me. I expect nothing from you, not even a reply if you wish; please remember that. Yesterday in class when I saw your name on my attendance I had recognized it and then when I saw you, well you truly are the spitting image of a woman I once knew. Her name was Alice Spencer, we went to school together, and she later married a man named Eli Harris who if I am correct is your father. Please are you really Alice's daughter? I believe you are; you'd have to be with your eyes, I thought I was seeing Alice when I saw you at first. Her soul, essence; you probably have her spirit too, or something close, but definitely her eyes. I would like to believe I would be able to recognize Alice's daughter; Alice sent me a picture of her daughter once, she would have been four or five in the picture. I dug out that old photo and she looks just like you, it must be you.

I want to apologize for what happened to Alice, I had received news of her death and it truly pained me to hear of it, and then of course what happened to your father. Eli's trial was all over the news 'Man Tries to Murder Daughter in Her Sleep for Looking like Deceased Wife.' Front page stuff. That must have been a horrifying and painful time for you. Then of course having to move away from the only home you've ever known, I had no idea that you came to Babylon though.

My only wish in sending you this letter is to confirm my suspicions that you are the daughter of Alice Harris. I cannot be sure of how much you know of your mother's school days or if you know anything at all. We were close once your mother and I and I only wish to pay my respects to you for what happened. Take from this what you may; I know you don't owe me anything but if you are inclined I'd appreciate it if you put my mind at ease and grant me the knowledge I've inquired about.

A. Knox

I put the letter down on a pillow next to me and was in awe, all my suspicions were right; Mr. Knox and I were on the same wavelength. Scary thought. How to proceed? I could use this to my advantage, get him to tell me the things my mother never would, get his side of all her stories. My thoughts curled in my mind, all the missing pieces of my mother's life that I longed for. I could find out how my mother ended up with my father, what happened between her and Mr. Knox? He could tell me everything I wanted to know and perhaps he had similar questions for me? What happened to my mother after they parted? What her life was like with my father and me? The possibility of exchanging information was tempting, very tempting."

Chapter Four: Waiting

Dr. Wiseman just sat and stared at Gabriella. Saving her was definitely going to be a challenge; a mother who committed suicide, a schizophrenic father who tried murdering his own daughter in her sleep; and he could only imagine what's taken place between Mr. Knox and herself since that first letter. That worried him. Dr. Wiseman was running everything in his mind when he glanced at his watch realized their hour was almost up. He brought his focus back to finish their session.

"Well, Miss. Harris I think we have made a very good start and you've certainly given me quite a lot to think about. I assume you are the daughter Mr. Knox was referring to and that you told him so."

"Yes. I wouldn't have much of a story to tell otherwise would I" Gabriella chuckled slightly, "and I certainly would not be in my current situation."

"Right," Dr. Wiseman needed to take in Gabriella's last words. "You certainly have been through quite a lot for one so young."

"It's all in the hand you're dealt, I guess," Gabriella smiled at Dr. Wiseman and rose from his couch, "So when would you like me to come back?"

Dr. Wiseman did not want to wait a whole week to hear more of Gabriella's story, so he told her Thursday at four would be great. That would give him a couple days to process the first part of her tale. Gabriella agreed, shook Dr. Wiseman's hand and left his office leaving him with his thoughts.

On Gabriella's way out she stopped in front of the second photograph to admire it, and to give herself a chance to organize her thoughts. Luckily, for her Dr. Wiseman's waiting room was empty.

"Well that went well... I think?" she said to herself, "I didn't bolt this time, he seems alright, he listened, even seemed concerned at some points." Gabriella had to take a deep breath to settle herself.

"I did the right thing," she said to the photograph, "I'm doing the right thing." After she seemed to settle herself down a bit she left Dr. Wiseman's waiting room checking her watch ensuring she had enough time to get to her favorite little coffee shop.

It was just after eleven when Gabriella finally got home. Her Aunt Enid and Uncle John had already retired to their room so she didn't have to sneak past them; once they went to bed, they were dead to the world. Gabriella went to the kitchen to make a quick peanut butter and jam sandwich and headed up to her room.

Gabriella's room was very eclectic, she liked too many different things; she couldn't choose which way to style her room so she put a little bit of everything on her walls. Gabriella's walls were white because her aunt wouldn't let her paint them so she had posters, flags, and art all over her walls. A Bond poster, Marilyn Monroe, Singing in the Rain, South Pacific, The Full Monty and Doctor Who; posters of The Beatles and Sting; on the wall above her bed she had half a dozen flags from different countries. Gabriella was determined to get a flag of every country. Around the room, Gabriella had a couple of large bookshelves overflowing with books, from Shakespeare's plays all the way to the Harry Potter books. Gabriella enjoyed reading everything, every genre, topic, from history to mythology, fantasy to mystery; she even had a spot for some old comic books she still owned.

Gabriella didn't have a lot of clutter in her room; everything was organized and kept in its place. Her guitar in the far corner, her bed always made, clothes folded away in her armoire, her desk was never messy, she had a cup that held her pens and pencils, and she usually had a book lying open on top as well as another book on her bedside table, for when she couldn't sleep.

Gabriella set her bag down next to her desk as she entered her room, sat on her bed and ate her peanut butter and jam sandwich while deep in thought about all she had done throughout the day. She was thinking of the one-step forward, two steps back scenario. Gabriella had certainly taken a step forward but then took two huge steps back.

When Gabriella had finished eating, she turned her radio on for some background music then opened her closet to gain access to her haven. Gabriella kept her most precious things hidden up there; she pulled the small ladder down and climbed up. Gabriella felt like she could breathe again, now she was home. Gabriella spent most of her nights hidden away in her haven; she had enough pillows and blankets up there that she was always comfortable. She had everything she needed. Gabriella reached for Shakespeare's A Midsummer Night's Dream and pulled out a stack of letters tucked away in it. She nestled in and read every letter from the first to the last slowly absorbing all they held. She fell asleep reading her letters.

At six in the morning, Gabriella's alarm clock next to her bed went off. She woke, quickly put her letters back in A Midsummer's Night's Dream and climbed down to shut off her alarm. Gabriella started her day off the same as always, showered, dressed and gathered all her schoolbooks. By seven, she was together and ready to go meet David for breakfast at the local diner; they had breakfast there every Tuesday. It only takes Gabriella fifteen minutes to walk to the diner and only a ten-minute walk from there to the high school. Gabriella did the routine saying good morning to her aunt and uncle who were in the kitchen. Uncle John sitting at the table reading the morning paper while Aunt Enid was busy making his eggs. Gabriella headed for the front door when Aunt Enid stopped her.

"I didn't hear you come home last night... when did you get in?" Aunt Enid didn't believe in private matters; but she did believe that everything was her business.

"Oh yeah I was a bit late sorry, David and I were working on a project for science," Gabriella gave her aunt her 'stay out of my business' smile then quickly left before her aunt could say anything more.

David was already waiting for Gabriella when she got to the diner, and he had already ordered their breakfast.

"Hey... our food will be right out," he said smiling as Gabriella sat next to him.

"Great," she replied.

"So what happened to you yesterday after school...? I thought we were going to hang out?" Their food arrived as David finished asking his question.

"Yeah sorry I forgot to mention I had a doctor's appointment after school. I meant to tell you I couldn't come over, must have slipped my mind. I'm sorry," Gabriella gave David a small smile then started to eat her breakfast.

"Oh... that's OK... is everything alright?" David could always worry.

"Yeah everything's fine; just a checkup, nothing to worry about." With another reassuring smile to David, they carried on with their breakfast.

The rest of the day went along the same as always. Classes, lunch, more classes then school was done for the day. Gabriella and David hung out in his garage for a bit, David was rebuilding an old mini; he always liked talking to Gabriella as he fixed it, trying to explain everything to her, she never could understand how cars worked, she only knew how to drive one.

At six Gabriella was back home having dinner with her aunt and uncle trying it ignore all her aunt's annoying questions on how her day was. Then she was back up in her room, alone and happy. Around eight when Gabriella could hear the television on in the den downstairs she opened her bedroom window, climbed down and out of the house off to her favorite coffee shop.

Gabriella had created a routine life for herself; she didn't enjoy change very often and always tried to keep to her routine without too many interruptions; so Wednesday went along very similar to the day before. School, David, dinner and her favorite coffee shop; and Thursday morning followed her same routine, but when school was done instead of going to David's she headed to Dr. Wiseman's office, giving David some excuse why she couldn't come over.

Chapter Five: Corresponding

Gabriella made it to Dr. Wiseman's office with ten minutes to spare. She didn't mind so much. It gave her time to admire his photograph again. She was trying to figure out why she liked that middle photo so much, why it intrigued her more than the others. The extra ten minutes also gave Gabriella a chance to remember where she stopped on Monday and where to pick up her story.

A couple minutes to four a man, thin and lanky stepped out of Dr. Wiseman's office. He looked like a businessman to Gabriella. He wore a nice suit and shiny black shoes and carried a briefcase. He didn't look at Gabriella as he walked quickly by, he kept his head down and it sounded like he was muttering to himself but Gabriella couldn't make any of it out. He walked out the door just as Dr. Wiseman got to his office door and said hello to Gabriella motioning for her to come in. Dr. Wiseman took his place in his chair as Gabriella sat down on his cushy couch then Dr. Wiseman started off their session.

"So how are you? How were the last couple of days?"

"I'm good, everything was routine as always. You know school, friends, that sort of thing, and you? How are you?"

"Oh, I'm good." Dr. Wiseman smiled, "so routine? Do you have a lot of routines?" he was curious to know more of her lifestyle. He could sense that Gabriella did not have a very spontaneous nature.

"Ah... yes, I have a very set routine for just about everything really; after everything I... I don't like change very much." Gabriella looked down to his grey carpet instead of looking at Dr. Wiseman.

"Yes, well that's perfectly normal," Dr. Wiseman, replied in hopes of encouragement toward Gabriella.

Gabriella looked back up from the carpet as Dr. Wiseman continued to talk.

"So shall we pick back up from where we left off on Monday?"

Gabriella gave a small nod then continued with her story.

"So Mr. Knox had given me a letter asking about whom I was, my parents. I didn't know what to do, what I wanted and I had no one to talk to about it either. This was not something I could tell David because I never told him my past.

It had been two weeks now since Mr. Knox had given me the letter; and I still hadn't made my mind up about it, I had decided to keep my distance from Mr. Knox until I could really make a decision. I felt for David though, the whole time he could tell there was something bothering me and occupying my mind but I couldn't bring myself to tell him, there would be too many questions on top of the many questions I already had. I didn't need or want more. David never stopped asking though, always wanting to know why Mr. Knox and I would never look eye to eye and when we did actually speak to each other it was always very short and awkward. Finally, David had had enough of all my clandestine behaviour and he showed up in my room, cornered me and tried to get me to tell him what was going on.

"Gabs come on now, what's going on with you? What's going on inside that head of yours? And what is going on between you and Mr. Knox? The two of you never look at each other; I mean the first day of class he couldn't take his eyes off you and what; now he can't stand the sight of you? So tell me." He was angry, angry that I was keeping things from him. He also had a proud aloof surrounding him for doing what he felt was necessary; how could I deny him what he wanted to know? How? I hated keeping things from David; after all, he was my only friend. I knew he wasn't going to believe anything but the truth so I told David to wait a minute, I went up to my haven, grabbed Mr. Knox's letter, climbed back down and handed it to David. He took his time reading it as I had; taking everything in.

"Wow... wow!" was all David could get out after reading the letter; he dropped it on my bed.

"Really? So you told him... you told him and that's why everything is so awkward?" he wanted to know what Mr. Knox wanted to know. It was all over his face; after all, I never told David about my parents, about what happened. I just told him they had died and my aunt and uncle took me in. I could see that he was not going to drop this. He left me no choice; I had to tell him.

"David, I haven't replied to him," I had to take a breath, "because, well he's right; about everything. Alice Harris was my mother and everything he said about my father... was true... he tried to... well, it's all true... and I... I just don't know if I want to or if I'm even ready to face everything yet." I went silent to let David take everything in before continuing.

"Now you know, my mother killed herself and my father's locked up for trying to murder me. That's my life and it's not something I want everyone to know about. I'm sorry I didn't tell you but I couldn't. I just couldn't."

David stared at me in shock. I sat down on my bed to wait for David to take in everything. After a minute, he sat down next to me and said, "Start from the beginning."

I shook my head, I couldn't tell him. Talk about my past, my parents, and I didn't believe he needed to know. David knowing wouldn't change anything and I was afraid he'd see me differently. I simply said he knew the important things already, my mother's suicide and my father's incarceration and that the rest was ancient history. David finally let it go and after he left I grabbed a piece of paper, sat back down on my bed, and started to write. I knew I would never be able to actually talk to Mr. Knox about his letter so I decided to write him his own.

Mr. Knox,

I know you wrote me a couple weeks ago inquiring to who I am, I am in fact the daughter of Alice Harris; your intuition was correct.

Please forgive me for taking so long in replying to you, it's just I needed time to process your letter. I'm convinced that once reading this you too will need time to process.

Thank-you for your condolences regarding the death of my mother; and what happened regarding my father.

I have to admit that I recognize you that first day in English too, it took me a minute to figure out how I knew you but once I did, you couldn't have been anyone else. I recognized you from my mother's photo album, and once you said your name I knew was right. My mother used to tell me all about the two of you, while we flipped through the photo album. I had no idea that she sent you a photo of me, but then my mother did have many secrets. She never would tell me what happened between the two of you, why she stopped seeing you. I suppose it shouldn't really surprise me that even though she didn't see you anymore that it didn't mean she didn't stay in touch from time to time.

I moved to Babylon just after my father was sent to the Ridgefield Mental Institution. My aunt and uncle got full custody of me and Babylon is where they live. It wasn't actually that hard moving here, I didn't have much of a life back home, no friends, no parents; moving was the least of my pains. As to my pains yes my father's attack was horrifying as you put it; as was my mother's suicide but I do believe that over time my wounds will heal. I hope.

Sincerely,
Gabriella Harris

I folded up my letter to Mr. Knox and sealed it into an envelope then tucked it away in my book bag. I couldn't sleep that night, thinking about the letter. I knew that giving Mr. Knox the letter was the right thing to do; he deserved the truth as David did. My fear of knowing the truth is what kept holding me back, once Mr. Knox knew then he'd ask questions and we'd have to talk about my mother, my life, we'd talk about the things I'd been trying to block out of my mind, and that scared me, scared me to my very core. I was not looking forward to school the next morning; arguing repeatedly in my mind on whether or not to give Mr. Knox the letter; I had until the last class of the day to decide. David didn't help much, he kept telling me to tell Mr. Knox, saying he had a right to know. David was right of course but that didn't stop me from fighting it and by the end of English, I had finally made up my mind on what to do. I stayed glued to my seat while my classmates left the room, David gave me this 'it's going to be okay' look before fully leaving the room; he understood that this was something I needed to do myself. It took me a minute to gather up the courage to pull out my letter to give Mr. Knox, but before I could stand and give it to him, he spoke.

"Miss Harris, you're still here?" he sounded surprised to see me still sitting at my desk; "Is there something I can do for you?" he tried to sound very nonchalant as he spoke to me.

I stood from my seat and held out my hand with the letter for him, I didn't say anything I just waited for him to take it; then I grabbed my bag and headed for the door. He said, "Wait" and I just stopped at the edge of the door and turned back to look at him. I still didn't speak but neither did he. We stood there for a couple of seconds staring at each other before I finally spoke.

"Please... just read it... you'll understand after you read it... I hope."

"Stay," he started, "stay, talk I'll... I'll read your letter just stay so we can talk about it... that is if it says what I think it does." He looked so hopeful, that feeling after all this time he'd finally find what he'd been looking for. He looked at me as if I was an answer he had been searching for; I didn't want to stay; I wanted to run, run far away from him. I didn't know why though, I had the strangest feeling about Mr. Knox, something I'd never felt before. I was always flushed around him; I knew he was off limits, after all, he was my mother's old friend, lover, or something; he was married, older than myself, and above everything my teacher. I did not want to be that girl; the girl that had a thing for her teacher, I didn't want to be the cliché. I certainly found him attractive though, his accent. I needed to get of that room but he had such a hopeful look on his face. I had no idea what was going on inside his head.

"I... I... I can't. Sorry. Just read it. Please." I didn't give him a chance to speak; I left his classroom as quickly as I could. I figured he'd try to talk to me about my letter tomorrow and I was fine with that but right in that moment I couldn't stay there and talk about everything, answering his questions that I knew he'd have. I realize that just because I was able to tell Mr. Knox the truth about who I was, it did not mean I was ready to actually talk about it. I didn't know how long Mr. Knox stood there holding my letter. But I do know he was happy with what it said."

Gabriella stopped talking and looked up at Dr. Wiseman; she got up off his couch and started to wander his office. She studied all the books overflowing on his bookshelves; most of them were psychology books from when he was in school Gabriella imagined. Some art books, he seemed to have a book for just about every subject. Gabriella took notice of his second bookshelf, which only had one genre of books on it. They were all his religious books, different types of Bibles and reference books, some novels but not by any authors Gabriella had ever heard of. On the very bottom shelf, there were a few children's books. Dr. Wiseman followed Gabriella with his eyes, watching where she chose to look and what caught her attention the most. He was pleased that his religious section caught her.

"Are you alright, Miss. Harris?" he thought he would ask for the sake of saying something, trying to understand her state of mind.

"Yes, I'm fine; nothing to worry about," Gabriella didn't look at him, she kept her gaze on all the books he had; she liked that he was a reader, had a large collection like herself. Once she was finished reading some of the titles of his books she returned to his cushy couch ready to continue.

"I was wrong, Mr. Knox didn't talk to me about my letter the next day, and in fact he hardly talked to me at all. I did catch him looking at me a bit more but I figure he was now trying to figure me out. The next few days were hard, more awkward then I would have expected; Mr. Knox clearly found it to be the same way. He wasn't sure how to see me anymore, student or daughter of an old friend? I mean the man had a picture of me from when I was five; it had to make him think. I felt for David, he was the only other person who knew what was going on so he kind of got caught in the middle. I did tell David about informing Mr. Knox through a letter instead of an actual conversation, and that we still hadn't actually talked about everything. I could tell David wanted to protect me and be there every step of the way; but he also knew that I needed space with this.

It was about a week before Mr. Knox responded to my letter; he didn't keep me after class as I thought but instead he wrote to me again. He tucked it in with the assignment he was handing back. He still didn't talk to me but he was definitely watching me more closely and I noticed that he was smiling a lot more. I again kept his letter tucked out of sight even from David, I figured I'd tell David; I just wanted to know what it said first. So when I got home that day I locked myself in my room, climbed up into my haven and read Mr. Knox's second letter:

Miss. Harris,

Thank you for telling me who you are. You were right in leaving last week when I asked you to stay. I needed time to read your letter a few times before actually believing it. I mean I believed it but it took a couple of times before it truly sunk in. You have to understand that I've been thinking of you since I found out about you. Alice's daughter; I imagined her to be just like Alice and for the most part, you are. I see so much of her in you, the way you write, how you are with people. It's almost like Alice's soul is with you.

I have to say I'm glad you knew who I was that first day in class. I'm surprised that Alice told you about me at all but I can't say I wasn't happy about that. Alice and I used to be very close; only ever friends if you were thinking we were anything more. I did love her though, your mother; it was hard not to love her. I know your mother didn't tell you how or why we parted but if you'd like to know, I don't see why I couldn't tell you at this point. The past is the past nothing will change that. I suppose you know that better than anyone. I am sorry that you've had such a hard life and from what you said in your letter, it's been quite a lonely one. If you ever wanted to talk, I'm here. I'm more than happy to see you and discuss your mother or anything really. I'd love to get to know you, find out just how much like Alice you are. I'm sure you have questions about her; I know I have some questions for you. What was she like as a mother? How things were between her and your father? Nevertheless, these are just some of my curiosities; I really just want to make sure she was loved. You don't have to tell me anything if you don't want to and you don't need to indulge me either. If you want to keep everything in the past I will respect that; I simply thought it would be nice for both of us to get a little clarity about the women we both knew and loved.

Sincerely,
A. Knox

I read the letter again a couple of times before hiding it with the other one, inside Shakespeare's A Midsummer's Night's Dream. I stayed locked up in my haven for the rest of the night thinking about Mr. Knox's newest letter to me. I was right in what he would want after he found out. He was clearly more in love with my mother than she seemed to be with him. He was willing to tell me the end of their story. I now had to decide if I was ready for this, if I really wanted to know. I could just put Mr. Knox's mind at ease, tell him about my mother being a mother, how my parents were together, but talking about my parents wasn't something I did and what would happen if I did tell Mr. Knox all about my childhood? My parents? I already had a 'school crush' on him and spending all that time alone with him wouldn't help with that. So I spent all this time with Mr. Knox, let him get to know me, maybe get to know him a bit and then what, never see him again after we run out of stories about my mother? That's really what he wants, my mother.

I fell asleep in my haven that night thinking everything through; the alarm next to my bed woke me the next morning telling me it was time to get up. My night of thinking did nothing for me; and I was just as confused in the morning than I had been the night before. I had breakfast and headed for school, meeting David halfway as usual. I didn't tell him about Mr. Knox's newest letter and I acted as though I never received it. David did ask me about Mr. Knox, he couldn't help himself but I lied to him. David decided Mr. Knox needed time to process my letter and he'd talk to me when he was ready. We got to school and I tried to act like there was nothing on my mind. It was even harder to do once we got to English class.

Mr. Knox had this hopeless look on his face again whenever he looked in my direction and all I could do was sink down into my seat. I needed to get him out of my mind; and I definitely need to get over my crush on him. I mean what was I thinking? He'd never go for me, he's married and he was completely in love with my mother. I tried to ignore him as he taught the class. The bell finally rang but as I went to leave, Mr. Knox called my name asking me to wait a minute. I told David to go on ahead as I walked over to Mr. Knox ignoring the looks from my classmates as they moved passed me. I already knew what he wanted; he wanted an answer to his letter; problem was I still didn't have an answer for him, I hadn't decided what I wanted yet.

"So," he started as he watched his last student leave his classroom. "So... um... have you..." but I cut him off.

"Look, sorry but I, I need to think about all this. I don't know if I'm ready for the rest of my mother's story." I found it difficult standing before him saying no. "I know that there's stuff you want to know but talking about my family is not something I've ever been comfortable with so I'm gonna need some time."

I didn't give Mr. Knox a chance to respond, I high-tailed it out of his classroom and caught up with David; he was waiting just down the hall for me.

"So, what did he want?" David wasted no time in interrogating me. Since I hadn't told David about Mr. Knox's second letter I told him that Mr. Knox wanted to talk about my letter but I wasn't ready to, David looked disappointed after that but stopped questioning me.

Mr. Knox's letter, what I said to him was stuck in my head for the next few days. I kept trying to distract myself with my homework but I couldn't. Mr. Knox had completely taken over my mind and that's when I made my decision, it was time. So late one night curled up in my haven I wrote to Mr. Knox:

Mr. Knox,

I know that I said I needed time with everything; your offer to share the rest of my mother's story and I do, need time; however I can't seem to think about anything else. I am curious to know how my mother ended up with my father, how they met? I suppose you know. What happened between the two of you? Why she stopped seeing you? I know there are things you'd like to know as well, so if you'd like we could find a way to swap stories as it is. I'm not sure how to proceed here? Not wanting to give people the wrong impression. I'll let you decide on how we should go about this.

Sincerely,
Gabriella Harris

I tucked my note to Mr. Knox in my English assignment; then continued on with the rest of my homework. I felt a bit more at ease, finally making my mind up. I went to bed that night ready to finally know the end of my mother's story."

Chapter Six: Meeting

Dr. Wiseman sat listening intensely to Gabriella's story; he knew some parts would be more important than other would but he didn't want to miss anything just in case. Gabriella continued.

"David could tell l was in a better mood that morning, which of course made him happy. l noticed with David how if l was down or if there was something going on with me, he would always shadow my mood. The sign of a true friend l imagine. He asked me what was up, why my spirits were good so l told him l was ready to talk to Mr. Knox about my mother. We got to school and went about our normal routine. Math, history, gym, then lunch followed by science and English. Normally l didn't look forward to English, my fear of seeing Mr. Knox but with my mind clear and made up l didn't mind so much.

After Mr. Knox collected our homework and my note was securely with him l stopped stressing and decided to enjoy class. Everyone went to independent reading, while l and most of the female class discreetly eyed Mr. Knox as he flipped through everyone's homework until coming across mine; see the note and start to read it. l was a bit shocked, l figured he'd be a bit more discrete about it, but there he was standing at the front of the classroom reading my note. You could just see the loose note poking out the top of my assignment; l found that slightly risky seeing how the majority of the girls were staring at him as l was. He looked up from my note and smiled; l thought he'd be happy with what it said. Some of the other female students followed Mr. Knox's gaze over to me and I could see their annoyed expressions from the corner of my eye. It worried me slightly, I didn't want people to start talking about Mr. Knox and myself again but at the same time seeing him smile at me made me not care what everyone else thought.

Mr. Knox returned to his desk and remained there until the bell went. I could feel his eyes on me throughout the rest of the class. At the sound of the bell, Mr. Knox came up to my desk asking me quietly if I could stay a minute. David noticed and I could see him go uneasy; David knew I had to talk to Mr. Knox and he definitely wanted me to tell him my mother's story once I learnt the rest of it but he hated the idea of me being alone with Mr. Knox. I nodded to Mr. Knox agreeing to stay when Mr. Knox sat back down at his desk, I turned to David telling him to go ahead and that I'd see him tomorrow. David protested saying he'd wait but I didn't know how long Mr. Knox and I would be and I really didn't want him to. I knew if David waited that as soon as Mr. Knox and I were done he would bombard me with questions and I didn't want that, I'd want to go over our conversation and take time to process everything, not relay it moments after. I told David not to worry and that I'd see him later. So David sulked out of the classroom with everyone else leaving Mr. Knox and I alone.

I shifted in my seat to face Mr. Knox; we locked eyes for a minute or two before he got up from his desk to go shut the classroom door. I shifted again following him with my eyes, from his desk to the door, from the door to the seat next to me. It was a few seconds before either of us spoke; we were just kind of staring at each other as if we were in awe of each other. His stare went right through me. We knew about one another but now we were actually going to have that long overdue conversation regarding our pasts.

"Sorry," he broke the silence. "I've waited a long time for this." His accent always made me melt, I had to resist the urge to lean in and kiss him. I tried to focus again. "Like I told you I've wanted to know you since Alice told me about you." He went to his desk and grabbed a photo out of the drawer then sat back down next to me, handing me the picture. I recognized it immediately; it was me, sitting on my mother's lap. He was right I looked just like my mother and I looked to be around four or five years old, smiling, happy. I didn't see many pictures of myself, even before my mother died; my father wasn't big on 'family photos' so after she died I never had my picture taken. As I looked at the picture, I remembered how pretty I was; no scars, wide happy smile with a dimple on the right side of my smooth cheek. I was happy in that picture sitting on my mother's lap, her arms wrapped around me. She was happy too.

Mr. Knox watched as I examined the photo he handed me. "I love that picture; you and your mum, you both look so happy, so beautiful." He fell silent again, I looked up to him expecting to see him looking at me but he wasn't, his gaze was on my mother's face. "So beautiful," he said it quietly, I think he meant to say it in his head but it came out aloud.

"Yes. She was very beautiful," I said while placing the photo on my desk, "Very beautiful." I looked at him for another moment; he was still staring at my mother's face when I asked him a question.

"You were in love with her, weren't you?" It's all I asked but it was enough; Mr. Knox took his eyes of my mother and placed them back on me.

"She never loved me the way I loved her," he was sad as he said it, you could hear it in his voice.

"I... I wanted to marry Alice but she turned me down. That's well, that's the real reason we fell apart. I proposed during our second year of college but she had already met your father Eli at that point and I knew they were seeing each other but I figured it was now or never so, I took my chance. Alice told me that she had never seen me that way; she didn't want our friendship to change. Alice told me just how serious it was with Eli, and she wanted us to stay the same but I couldn't, I couldn't stay and watch her be with another man. I did try, I tried to like Eli and stay friends with them but in the end I had to walk away." Mr. Knox stopped to make sure I was keeping up which I was so I asked him a question, just to figure out the time line and all.

"So is that when you met your wife? When you walked away from my mother?" He nodded his head as he spoke.

"Yes, that's when I met Grace, my wife..." I watched Mr. Knox roll his wedding ring around his finger a few times, as he continued.

"Your mum made her choice and I had to move on. I did get a wedding invitation about a year later, I went with Grace, we were just dating at that point but I didn't want to watch your mum marry Eli alone. In the invitation, Alice wrote me a short note telling me how sorry she was for how we parted, and why. She said how much she would love to see me and what it would mean if I came to her wedding so I did and we were better after; we still didn't really see each other but we kept in touch from time to time. She told me about you, sent me the picture; but that was the last I heard from your mum, then Eli told me she had killed herself. He blamed me for Alice's suicide. Eli believed that I had confused her by talking to her again and that it would have been better for everyone if I had stayed away. I was already married to Grace at this point, about three years. I married Grace even though I loved your mum; but I couldn't be alone forever just because Alice didn't want me..."

I listened intensely as Mr. Knox told me about my parents, even about himself and his wife, Grace. He never fully loved Grace, but he married her anyway from what Mr. Knox told me. Grace loved him but at this point in their marriage, they were more like friends. The love and passion, the little there was, was gone and now their relationship was mostly out of convenience and fear of change. It was around five o'clock when the janitor came in to start cleaning when we realized just how long we had been sitting there talking. Well Mr. Knox was doing most of the talking which I really didn't mind."

Gabriella stopped again and looked up to Dr. Wiseman for a moment before continuing.

"You know that was the first honest conversation I ever had with Mr. Knox, the second one happened a few days later. Mr. Knox and I arranged to meet up one Saturday afternoon across town at this little coffee shop; it's normally pretty quiet, not a lot of people and no one from the school ever went there. It quickly became our place.

In our second conversation, I did most of the talking; how all my parents ever did was fight but I never knew about what. I told him how my mum was with me, all her stories, made up or real. Mr. Knox said she was always good at telling tales. He already knew about my father's attack on me so he didn't really ask me about my scars, which made me happy. But as I told him about my life he looked so hurt by everything, as though he was taking my pain personally. As we were sitting there, talking Mr. Knox gently took my hand, and I felt a surge go through my whole body and that urge to kiss him came back. His dark, honey-brown eyes bore into me and I had to remind myself to breath. Being so close to him was not helping my crush in any manor, but I simply couldn't bring myself to pull away from him.

So this became my new routine, coffee with Mr. Knox once a week across town. I told David and at first, he was okay with it but when he noticed we were doing this right to the end of the school year he started to get annoyed. He'd ask me what we even talked about at this point; we could only have so many conversations about my mother. I was very short with David, telling him it wasn't any of his business and left it at that. Even after school was out for summer Mr. Knox and I continued to meet, a bit more regularly during the summer but he wanted us to be careful so I still kept our coffees discreet. David knew of course but I could trust him not to say anything; so I didn't talk about coffee with Mr. Knox with David and he pretended he didn't know about them.

It amazed me on how much Mr. Knox and I had to talk about, how many interests we shared. Philosophy, history, literature, we could actually choose an author and discuss them until we had nothing more to say, then go on to another one and start all over. We'd talk film and music, we even ventured on politics a little. I liked talking to Mr. Knox, he got me in ways David never did, or couldn't. Of course spending all that time with Mr. Knox did not help with my crush on him. I wondered how much longer I could go on, but at the same time, I liked to think we had become friends. I couldn't see how my mother couldn't have loved him. With all the time I was spending with Mr. Knox I kept getting this odd feeling, I knew us spending so much time together wasn't the best thing to do and it was obvious that he was seeing my mother in me, which is why I think he kept coming back. I assumed Mr. Knox was trying to relive his time with my mother through me; and I would try to ignore that particular fact because I was enjoying my time with him so much, we were having the conversations I had longed for with David. When David talks it's always cars, or his parents, David never was into English or History like I was. So I was finally getting the conversations I had been longing for, and I wasn't quick in wanting to give them up."

Chapter Seven: Friendships

Gabriella stopped there, she had thought of a question for Dr. Wiseman but she wanted to word it right. She glanced out the window trying to find the right words.

"Dr. Wiseman, what makes you believe in God? What makes you think God actually exists?" her one question was really two and it was the best she could come up with while trying not to sound too abrupt or rude about the subject. Gabriella thought this would be a delicate subject so she wanted to be careful while Dr. Wiseman couldn't help but smile as he watched her wait anxiously for his answer; as if everything she was waiting for lied behind it. Dr. Wiseman got up from his chair and headed over to his bookshelf and grabbed a book off the shelf then headed back to where he had left Gabriella sitting. In his hands, he held a Bible and placed it in her lap saying:

"Read this and you'll get your answer." Dr. Wiseman took his seat, smiled and then continued

"Now you do not have to read it in any particular order, just open and read. Miss Harris there is no good way to answer your questions; God is different to and for everyone, there is no wrong way to believe in God; it's mostly having faith, faith that God will take care of you, he will always love and care and protect you, never forsake you in your time of need. This book, everything that has happened in my own life, the gifts he has given me, Gabriella I could tell you my testimony but we're here for you, not me. All I can say is God saved my life and I can only hope that one day you will allow him to save yours. You keep that, take it home and think about what I said." Dr. Wiseman sat deeper in his chair and took a breath overjoyed by Gabriella's interest.

Gabriella shuffled in her seat clutching the Bible in her hands considering what she heard, the thought that Dr. Wiseman could be right sent chills down her spine, and Gabriella didn't know what to think anymore. Could God really be what she needed? Could he be everything Gabriella had been searching for? Gabriella's mind continued to go round and round trying to understand it all. She thought that by coming to see Dr. Wiseman she would tell him her story, get a quick *'awe well that's too bad but if you do this and this you'll be fine.'* She had never expected to encounter God in her sessions and definitely did not expect to walk out with a Bible in her hands. Gabriella found little possibility of a book saving her life. Dr. Wiseman watched Gabriella's mind turn, this was new for him, to watch someone trying to decide if God was right for them. The silence in the room grew larger and larger, Gabriella didn't want to be the first to break it, still grasping the Bible in one hand and brushing the cover with the other; she finally stopped glancing down at the Bible and placed it on his coffee table that sat between them, Gabriella smiled slightly asking:

"So should I continue or is that all the time we have today?"

"No, you're good, keep going," Dr. Wiseman checked his watch as he said it then looking back to her; Gabriella went back to her story.

"So, with the tenth grade behind David and me, and the eleventh almost done, nothing really changed. David and I were back in a good place despite the fact Mr. Knox and I we're still enjoying each other's company outside of school, we had become quite good friends. I could tell David was jealous of Mr. Knox and he made his disapproval of our friendship quite clear.

At the end of grade eleven, David and his parents decided to travel for the summer holidays and David decided that I was going with them; he was not about to leave me for a whole summer alone with our English teacher. David had told me that Mr. Knox had this look in his eye that tweaked him the wrong way when it came to me. It was very clear that he did not trust Mr. Knox as far as he could throw him.

In the end, David won and I agreed to go; an entire summer travelling with David did mean no Mr. Knox and I wasn't sure how I was going to handle it. I had gotten so used to talking and seeing Mr. Knox so much, he gave me my intellectual conversation and I was going to miss that; and him. I went through all the pros and cons of my decision to go with David, but I felt it for the best in the end. I needed to show David that I hadn't replaced him.

The last day of school, just before summer I went and told Mr. Knox that David and I were going to Europe all summer, so we wouldn't see each other until I returned. The look on his face told me everything I needed to know, he felt the same way as David, jealous. Mr. Knox gave me a hug telling me to stay safe and have fun, to stay in touch with a friendly postcard from time to time. I agreed. Said goodbye and walked away from Mr. Knox for a while summer. I think it was a bit heart breaking actually, Mr. Knox had become this huge factor in my life and I wasn't sure how to survive without him yet; at the same time I was excited to spend the whole summer bashing around Europe with my best friend.

So David and I were off and at the last minute David told me that his parents suddenly changed their summer plans and were sending us on our own. I had the feeling David had set the whole thing up but I couldn't back out at that point.

Europe was spectacular, Rome, Italy, Paris, London, Amsterdam, every city, every place was beautiful. I kept my word to Mr. Knox and sent him a postcard from every city we visited. I found that David and I grew closer over our summer travels; Europe had given us more things to talk about. The two of us alone all summer seeing the beauties of the world, the museums and art, the sceneries; it was perfect. I could tell David never wanted it to end. We had so much fun, we saw everything we could, did every club and party we found in every town we visited. I loved being abroad, seeing the world with my best friend by my side, but I had to admit that I was happy when the summer ended and it was time to go home. I had missed Mr. Knox more than I thought I would have, but more importantly, I was excited for my final year of high school. I was one year away from my freedom and I couldn't wait.

David and I were back in London waiting for our flight to Babylon. I had sent Mr. Knox a last postcard the day before telling him of our return. David was getting tense again as we headed home. He had enjoyed the summer more than I had; it had only taken David two days into our trip to relax and forget about Mr. Knox; so I was discreet with all my postcards to him.

David's parents were waiting for us when our plane landed. They took us for dinner meeting up with my aunt and uncle so everyone could hear our travel stories. I found that as I sat with them all at dinner that David's mother and my aunt seemed to be waiting for news, waiting for me to make some big statement that I never made.

Everything seemed to be going back into place once David and I returned. School was starting soon so we were getting ready for our final year as we fell back into our regular routines. I was glad that David hadn't turned completely sour since our return, the only thing that was worrying me was the fact that I hadn't heard from Mr. Knox yet. He had been so adamant about me keeping in touch over the summer and now, nothing. It had been a whole week since my return; I knew I would seem him once school started but I was anxious to see him again and I didn't really want to wait for school.

David had reviewed our timetables, we had the same classes together as usual and Mr. Knox was once again our English teacher but when we showed up to class he was nowhere to be seen. A woman named Ms. Godarsh was sitting at his desk prepping for the class. That had done it for my day; I was sour for the rest of it while David's spirits seemed to have lifted immensely. I hardly cared how happy David was, I hadn't seen or heard from Mr. Knox and now he wasn't even at school. I was worried and there was absolutely nothing I could do about it.

English class had become unbearable for me. I despised Ms. Godarsh, she had absolutely no interest in English, and there was no passion or heart when she taught. She was certainly no Mr. Knox, when Mr. Knox taught you could feel the words, the poetry, and the love and suffering of a character; Mr. Knox had the ability to completely captivate his entire class and really pull them into the depths of the work. Ten minutes listening to Ms. Godarsh and everyone was asleep. She was horrid, no true respect for what she was teaching, she was boring and spoke in the dullest monotone voice I had ever had the misfortune of hearing; and we were stuck with her until the Christmas break. Mr. Knox was supposed to return after the holiday. That was all I was able to find out about Mr. Knox's absence.

So I silently suffered as my life went back the way it was before Mr. Knox came into it. On the other side of things, David was absolutely ecstatic with having me all to himself again.

The first couple of weeks were hard, I hadn't quite realized how much I had come to depend on Mr. Knox, how our conversations got me through my week. To go back to the same old same old with David I found it lacking, knowing that there was more; other people who could hold my conversational interests more than David ever could. It wasn't that David wasn't intelligent enough he simply had few interests.

My spirits began to rise on our last day of school before the Christmas break. It was Ms. Godarsh's last day and that meant Mr. Knox would be back before I knew it. I had asked around about where Mr. Knox was but all anyone would say was that he took a sabbatical.

My anticipation for the return of school made me feel like every day had been set on slow. David was of course by my side every day of the break. He had started on a new project in his garage so our days were spent in there listening to music as I watched David work. I figured watching David work on another car was as good as anything to keep my mind off Mr. Knox and I had noticed watching David work how much he'd changed, he wasn't the scrawny, pale boy I had first met; he had started to fill out and buff up from working on car after car.

When school came back in and I saw Mr. Knox wandering the school halls I knew that everything had finally gone back to normal. I was excited to renew my friendship with Mr. Knox, to graduate, and to let life take me where it may. When English class started, I had the oddest feeling there was something off with Mr. Knox; I just didn't know what. I could tell there was something amiss with him; not that he had been ill but there was something, something had happened and that something was not a good something. Mr. Knox seemed out of sorts, his spirit was not what it had been before I left for the summer. He completely avoided me I didn't get it. I mean yes we kept our friendship 'hushed up' at school but he would still acknowledge me. Before I left he was jealous and making sure I would stay in touch with him but now, he was completely different. What had happened? Now it was as if he couldn't even stand the sight of me. It bothered me greatly that I couldn't figure it out, what was Mr. Knox's problem.

David on the other hand was overjoyed by how Mr. Knox was behaving, not giving me any attention unlike before. It was as if Mr. Knox had become a completely different person; it saddened me but what could I do, really? My heart broke that day. I stayed late after class to talk to Mr. Knox, find out what was going on. All he said was that we couldn't see each other anymore; that we needed to strictly have a student teacher relationship and not be friends outside of school anymore. He did not wait for me to respond, he walked out of his classroom leaving me shocked and confused. What could have happened?

I told David what Mr. Knox had said, I was more upset about losing Mr. Knox than I should have been but I didn't care; to be honest I never thought I'd actually ever lose him. David tried to be a friend about the whole thing but I could see the happiness in his eyes and that made it harder. Yes, I knew David never liked Mr. Knox but we had bonded in a way that I didn't actually understand at the time; but I certainly felt that emptiness Mr. Knox's absence now left.

Another month passed and Mr. Knox and I were hardly speaking. I rarely needed help with the assignments he gave out so I had no reason to speak to him, we'd do the pleasant 'Hi, how are you today' thing but it was hardly the same. I think he felt it too; sometimes I'd catch him staring at me. When that happened I would always feel a bit better about the whole thing because it told me it was something that was keeping us apart. Something had happened over the summer that kept him from returning to school right away, that was keeping us from the friendship we had formed over the last two years. My curiosity kept eating away at me. David would tell me to move on, forget him but he never did understand that I couldn't. Mr. Knox and I had connected, we understood each other better than anyone else would or could ever understand us; David couldn't see that. It pained me to realize that Mr. Knox understood me far better than David ever could. I decided that I wanted, that I deserved an explanation from Mr. Knox. After the month of not speaking to him, I simply could not take it anymore. I did the one thing I could. The one thing I knew he could not ignore. So as I sat in my history class I wrote Mr. Knox a letter.

Mr. Knox,

For the most part, I can respect your choice to terminate our friendship; however, I do believe that I have the right, that I deserve an explanation for your decision. I'm sorry if this makes you uncomfortable but I would like to know. If I have done something or if something has happened then please just tell me, we can talk about this. Forgive me for asking but, what did keep you from returning to school after the summer? I'm curious to know if the reason for your absence is the same for your ending our friendship. I understand that may sound very self-centered, making it sound like any reason you have will relate to me in some way but I can assure you that I do not intend it that way. If you simply no longer have interest in keeping company with me then fine. I can accept that and your absence is none of my business; and well, I can accept that too. I do not mean to sound self-centered in any way I'm simply very confused. Before summer you seemed upset of my going to Europe with David, asking me to stay in touch, not wanting me to forget you; and I did. When I came home, you wanted nothing to do with me so I think I have the right to be confused along with the right to a few answers. I do believe you owe me at least that much. I will take the chance of upsetting you and I promise that I will never bother you again once I know. I will be at our coffee shop today after school around four thirty, please meet me there and talk to me. Help me understand what is going on, I know that I shouldn't, but I miss you. I miss our conversations, spending time with you; I miss my friend. So please I am asking not only as my friend but also as my mother's old friend, please talk to me.

Sincerely,
Gabs

I folded my letter up and tucked it into my book bag. When the bell went I grabbed my things impatient to get to English, I was only a couple minutes early before the second bell; Mr. Knox was sitting at his desk. Other students started to fill in so I took my seat, anxious to give Mr.

Knox the letter. I was agitated the whole class, wanting to give him the letter. David tried to talk to me but I didn't want to hear anything he had to say. I tried to pay attention to the lesson but my mind wouldn't let me. The hour went by so slowly but when it was over, I discretely put the letter on Mr. Knox's desk and left ignoring David's looks as I walked away. David caught up to me in the hallway and pulled me aside.

"Hey, what was that you put on Mr. Knox's desk? I thought you two weren't talking anymore?" David had noticed the letter, of course he had, he'd been watching me closely these days, keeping an eye on me. He believed he was doing it for my own good but I wasn't buying it.

"It's nothing David, honest. I... I just want an explanation from him, that's all." I walked away leaving David looking unimpressed in the hallway. I needed to get across town and wait for Mr. Knox. I'd imagine him reading my letter and agreeing with my request, calling his wife and telling her he'd be home late, then head out to meet me.

I sat and waited for Mr. Knox until the shop closed but he never came. He clearly wanted nothing to do with me, but the fact that he wouldn't even give me and explanation hurt me more than him not wanting me in his life anymore. I was too upset to go home so when the waitress told me I had to leave I just wandered the streets thinking everything over. Whenever I had something on my mind that I couldn't process easily, I would go and find a swing set.

The sun had set and I found myself at the old abandoned elementary school. The school has a playground that's not entirely safe to play on anymore so no one ever really goes there. I found that the swing set was still in moderately good condition so that's where I went to think about my pains. Ever since I was a little girl I have loved to swing, it makes me feel free. I found that no matter what was going on inside my head or what was happening in my life; none of it mattered while I was swinging high above the world. I love it because nothing can touch me while I'm swinging.

I had lost track of time and before I knew it, it was about two in the morning. I decided it was time to go home, my aunt would be freaking out but I hardly cared about that. Swinging helped a little but not enough to ease my anger. Once I got home I decided it would be safer if I didn't use the front door; I climbed into the house through my bedroom window avoiding my aunt, but I didn't hear her in the house so I figured I had gotten lucky and she was in bed. I tried to sleep but I was still far too angry even though I had little right to be. Mr. Knox owed me nothing, not really; he was my teacher, an old friend of my mothers and a married man. I should have known that our friendship couldn't last very long. Something would have eventually happened causing us to end our friendship, telling myself that helped ease my anger."

"Miss. Harris, Miss. Harris, Gabriella, Gabs, you still with me here?" Gabriella could hear Dr. Wiseman's voice echoing in the back of her mind, she had drifted off in her head again, remembering her childish act of demanding answers from Mr. Knox put a smile on Gabriella's face. Her youthful fantasy of herself and Mr. Knox made her laugh at herself. She could still hear Dr. Wiseman trying to get her attention, clearing his throat.

"Where did you go?" Dr. Wiseman had finally gotten Gabriella's attention but he was curious to know what made her smile.

"Sorry, Dr. Wiseman, I, um, thinking about my reaction to Mr. Knox ending our friendship like that made me go off track; I guess." Gabriella fell back into her mind. So Gabriella and Dr. Wiseman just sat for a few seconds. Dr. Wiseman was trying to put himself in her shoes, she clearly had feelings for Mr. Knox but to have him suddenly end a two year friendship out of the blue, he would want answers too.

"Well Miss. Harris," Dr. Wiseman started, "I think that's a good place to leave it today." He hated to stop Gabriella's story, he wanted to hear the rest of it but he had other patients so Gabriella would have to wait.

"Monday? Same time?"

Gabriella agreed, shook Dr. Wiseman's hand and left not even bothering to admire her favourite photograph in his waiting room.

Chapter Eight: Secrets

Gabriella had gotten good at keeping secrets. When she first came to live with her aunt and uncle, Gabriella had little reason to lie or keep them; but since having Mr. Knox in her life, she's learnt to lie, to sneak around and to keep quiet. At first, she was only doing such things to her aunt and uncle, but then she started to lie and keep things from David. That was harder for Gabriella, she had never had a true friend before but she was sure that she was not treating David properly and Gabriella feared that her current actions might drive him away.

David knew a lot about Gabriella's relationship with Mr. Knox but there were things, important things, she wasn't telling him. Gabriella told herself she was withholding information for David's own good, she knew how much he despised Mr. Knox, and yes the things she kept from David he really didn't need to know but that left Gabriella with no one to share it with.

Gabriella put on a good facade with her everyday life, at home, at school; she started to feel that there were only two situations where she wasn't pretending anymore. When she was with Mr. Knox and when she saw Dr. Wiseman. They were the two people she didn't feel the need to be anything but herself with. The time spent away from either was tiring to her; keeping up her appearance of happiness. Gabriella still wasn't fooling David and she knew it, yet she still didn't have the strength to be honest with him.

Gabriella found herself spending less and less time with David, questioning their friendship, what was left of it. Gabriella no longer spent her weekends with David in his garage, watching him fix cars anymore. Gabriella found that once again her life was turned upside down and that everything was well out of control.

To Gabriella the weekend seemed to drag, she just wanted to be back sitting on Dr. Wiseman's couch telling him her story. So she occupied her time the best she could. Rereading her favourite Shakespeare play; Othello, finishing all her homework and even wrote a new song on her guitar; desperately trying to keep busy and out of trouble. So when four o'clock on Monday came around Gabriella was glad to be sitting in Dr. Wiseman's waiting room.

Gabriella watched the same lanky, suit-wearing, briefcase carrying man with his shiny black shoes coming out of Dr. Wiseman's office muttering to himself. She couldn't help but wonder about him; what his life was like? Why he was seeing Dr. Wiseman? Gabriella was daydreaming when Dr. Wiseman called her into his office. They took their regular seats and Dr. Wiseman started their session.

"Gabriella," he smiled as he started them off, "Did you have a good weekend?"

"I kept busy, you?" giving him a small smile in return.

"Good, it was good thank you. So we left off with you being stood up as it were. Mr. Knox never came to meet you?"

"Yes, that's right."

"Alright why don't you tell me what happened next," Dr. Wiseman sat back in his chair and allowed Gabriella to carry on in her tale.

"Well I didn't see anyone for a few days after that. I told my aunt that I wasn't feeling well and so I stayed home, away from the world. I was mad for a good couple of days; I was confused and hurt, didn't understand what had happened, why Mr. Knox chose not to meet me. My anger did lessen over the next few days. I couldn't look at Mr. Knox though; he didn't want me in his life so that's what I gave him. Every once in a while David would lean over to tell me Mr. Knox was staring at me but I told him I didn't care; even though I did. I finally convinced David that I didn't care about Mr. Knox in any way and it seemed to settle him a bit. I hated lying to David but I couldn't take his 'I'm so worried about you' looks anymore. It was about a week after I had given Mr. Knox the letter and me ignoring him that he finally tried to talk to me. I acted like a child and walked away from him, but before I could fully walk away from him though he handed me what looked like a letter.

My dearest Gabriella,

I am so sorry for the discomfort I've caused you and I will explain my actions to you of course. About half way through the summer when you were sending me the postcards, my wife found them. She confronted me about them, why a student was sending postcards to me from a summer vacation. She asked who you were and why you seemed to be so important to me. See, when you left for your trip, Grace and I well, we were trying to rekindle our marriage you could say. I was doing it for all the wrong reasons, but I'll get to that. I told Grace who you were, whose daughter you were. Finding out just who you were did not go over well with Grace.

Grace was always jealous of your mum, Alice, and now I was giving my time to her daughter. No matter what Grace did, she would never come first for me. As I told you before I married her, not truly loving her. Why do you think we have no children? I never wanted them with her. So after our very awkward conversation about you, Grace threatened me. I could agree never to see you again or she would report me to the school board telling them we were having an affair. I know that all we have is a friendship but even an accusation of an affair with a student would not only hurt my job but more importantly it would ruin your reputation and mark you as a student who sleeps around with the staff. I did not want that for you. I do ask your forgiveness, I want you in my life, more than you know but I will not destroy your reputation. You have been through so much grief and I didn't want to cause you anymore. It would appear that I have failed you in that anyways.

As to my absence at the beginning of the year, well Grace and I took an extended summer vacation. It was supposed to help us rekindle our marriage and get me away from you. I did hope that by rekindling my marriage it would get you out of my mind a bit. I won't say anymore on the matter. I wish things could be different but I don't want you getting hurt and my wife might just do what she threatens if I don't keep my distance. Please forgive me. I will forever keep you in my mind and consider you a very dear friend. Perhaps one day we can pick up where we left off but for now, I think this is best.

Your friend,
A. Knox

I was kicking myself after reading that. Knowing that I was right did nothing for me. He was protecting me; he didn't want me to be tainted. I read his letter a few more times through, reading his words knowing that he cared. I didn't like his wife very much, threatening that lie to the school board just because she was jealous. I could see her side in all this though. I thought that the most I could do was respect his position.

A couple of days went by and as hard as I tried I just couldn't let go of Mr. Knox's words so I decided we needed to talk in person, just before the end of class I scribbled down a quick

'Meet me at the abandoned park,
Eleven o'clock tonight. Need to talk.
Gabs'

After jotting down my note, I walked up to Mr. Knox sitting at his desk and dropped it right in front of him giving him no time to react; and before he had time to say anything I turned and walked right out of the classroom before the bell even went. I could feel David's eyes on me as I walked away; but I didn't care.

It was twenty to eleven so I decided it was time to slip out my bedroom window and head toward the park. I had no idea if Mr. Knox was going to show up or if he'd be able to slip out of the house without his wife catching him. My head was spinning; I couldn't keep anything in check. I thought if we could come to some happy medium, come to some conclusion. Maybe if we talk to Grace, explain how Mr. Knox and I were just friends, nothing more. I got to the park a few minutes early and with no sign of Mr. Knox, I went over to the swing-set and started to swing. I started singing while I let myself go on the swing-set.

'Oh I don't know what's reality?
Oh and I don't know what's fantasy?
I chose to believe that I live my dreams
And you, oh you're my reality
Oh my reality...'

I must have been singing too loudly because I never did hear Mr. Knox walk up to the swing-set. Once I saw him standing there I immediately stopped singing; no one had ever really head me sing, not because I had a bad voice but because I'm more of the shy type when it comes to a public display of oneself. I wondered what I must have looked like to him; this eighteen-year-old girl in the middle of the night singing her heart out while swinging on a swing-set like a five year old. The look on Mr. Knox's face told me everything. He looked like a man in complete awe, but more importantly, he looked like a man who was hooked. One more thing I got from my mother, her voice. I'm not sure how he did it but he actually looked happy and sad all at the same time. I could tell that he was kicking himself for coming but he was also glad that he had.

I slowed down my swing as Mr. Knox walked closer to where I was. I could see him shaking his head and when he came into earshot, I heard him ask.

"How am I ever supposed to walk away from you now?"

My swing had completely stopped at this point and he grabbed the one next to me. I didn't answer him, I just shrugged my shoulders; I wasn't sure how I was supposed to take his question so I took it more of a statement; or a question for himself he hadn't mean to say out loud. We just sat in silence for a moment, gently swaying back and forth on the swing-set.

"This isn't going to work is it?" he was asking even though we both knew he was right, as much as we wanted to be friends there would always be something standing between us.

"If we could just explain to your wife..." I started but he cut me off; he was shaking his head again. I was confused, his wife was what had been keeping our friendship on the shelf; I thought if we explained things but that wasn't what Mr. Knox wanted. He could see my confusion so he explained.

"Gabs, love, Grace is right in asking me to walk away from you; and she's right to suspect us of having more than friendship. You have to understand I married Grace while I was still in love with your mum and now... and now you," Mr. Knox fell silent and just stared at me. I finally clued in. He didn't want his wife. He wanted me.

I was infatuated with Mr. Knox; I wanted him just as much if not more than he wanted me. We worked, us together, the things we'd do, see and learn. I also thought of all the things I could learn from him; that was less important though. I liked him before I ever really knew him and now he only meant that much more to me. He started to lean closer to me and I could see where he was going. I reminded him of Grace, his wife; all Mr. Knox could do was nod and say 'I know' he never took his deep dark honey brown eyes off me. I don't think he could. As much as I was the daughter of the woman he had once loved so deeply; I believe he had fallen in love with me too, not just for the parts of me that were my mother; but for all of me. He had gotten to know the young woman in front of him and he couldn't walk away anymore. We sat in silence staring at each other for a while, that seemed to be the way with us, no words, not anymore, just silence. I don't know if it was the silence or the damp mist of the park but he turned back toward me and said, "Fuck it." Grabbing my swing and pulling me in close as his mouth found mine in a gentle kiss.

I wasn't entirely sure what to do. What was he to me at this point? Teacher? Friend? Could he now become my lover? So many things were going through my mind in that moment. I could feel his lips leave mine, and I knew he was disappointed. I looked up and caught his gaze, I could tell that he was about to say something but I didn't want him to. I made my mind up in that moment and just as he went to form his words, I leaned in further grabbing the collar of his blazer pulling him into me as I pressed my lips to his with more force then I meant. My forcefulness only seemed to urge him on as he pushed his tongue through my lips exploring my mouth fighting me for dominance. And I let him. Just like that, nothing left to say; I believed we had already said everything in the first two years of our relationship. I decided to stop thinking and simply embrace my surrounding. Our kiss seemed to last forever; time was irreverent in his arms. Nothing could touch us anymore, not his marriage; not the fact I was his student or the daughter of his first love. I was happy and safe in his arms and I never wanted to let go.

Mr. Knox grabbed my waist pulling me off the swing and lifting me up as he walked us over to the damp grass. I straddled him as he trailed hot kisses down my neck finding the pulse point and I could feel the bulge in his jeans grow larger, straining against the fabric. Spite the chill of the open air his body felt warm against mine. Mr. Knox reached up with one hand cupping my chin as we both attempted to catch our breaths. His honey-brown eyes were dark with lust, admiration.

"Mr. Knox..." I breathed out before he cut me off with another deep heated kiss.

My mind went completely blank as all I could feel was him. He moved his hands to the rim of my shirt lifting it up over my head and throwing it to the side exposing my black lacy bra to the air. I followed his lead having no idea what to do, I pulled at his grey blazer pushing it off of him and throwing it onto my shirt then started on the buttons of his mint-green collared shirt. Mr. Knox's shirt landed in the ever-growing pile of discarded clothing next to us as he lifted me off of him laying me down on the cold grass. Once on my back Mr. Knox trailed hot kisses down my neck and collarbone moving the fabric of my bra as his lips found my hardening nipples and I couldn't help the deep moan that escaped my lips. I bit down on my bottom lip failing to silence my moans. He reached around unclasping my bra as I moved to remove my jeans and shoes leaving me in nothing more than my black cotton panties. Mr. Knox's lips found mine again as my shacking hands reached for his jean button undoing them and tugging them down as his hands trickled down my flat stomach to my hips finding the rim of my panties. Once Mr. Knox's hands found my panties he slipped one under the fabric, gently rubbing the folds of my sex as another loud moan fell from my lips. He was making my whole body feel like it was on fire; my hips automatically moved to meet his hand as he dipped a finger inside rubbing my nub. Mr. Knox kissed me and I moaned again against his lips; I could feel him chuckle against me as my body was slowly starting to lose control.

Mr. Knox shifted again hovering over me as he slipped another finger between the folds of my now dripping sex as I moaned his name. He gazed down at me as his fingers picked up speed, watching me bite my bottom lip as I found myself coming closer to my climax. Mr. Knox leaned down finding my nipple again with his mouth, biting down causing me to call out in sweet pain.

"God I'm close" I breathed out as he moved to my other nipple while I run my hands threw his hair. Before I knew what was happening Mr. Knox's fingers left me as he went to fully remove his jeans and briefs as I removed my soaked panties leaving us both completely naked in the chilling grass.

My hands explored his lean body as Mr. Knox rubbed his full erect member against my now swollen sex. He moved to line himself up to my entrance and slowly pushed himself into me. We both moaned loudly at the contact. "Fuck" Mr. Knox breathed out as he slowly pulled himself out a bit before plunging even deeper and harder into me. We found our rhythm quickly as our bodies heated up against each other. I dug my nails into his back causing him to yell out in pain; grabbing my wrists and pinning them above my head; he ferociously kissed me. Our tongues explored each other's mouths again as he drove himself deeper and deeper inside of me. I could feel my body tightening around him and I knew I couldn't last much longer.

"God, harder, harder" I urged him on even more and he was more than willing to oblige. I found my release as Mr. Knox roughly plunged himself into me and my muscled tightened around his think member. Mr. Knox continued to move inside me as I rode the high of my climax as he followed spilling his warm seed inside me. We both stilled, panting, catching our breaths as our muscles started to relax and Mr. Knox showered me in gentle kisses before pulling himself away and laying down beside me. I felt the loss of him, already wanting him again but tiredness was quickly over taking the both of us.

I was wrapped in his arms, head on his chest as the air was filled with the sound of our heavy breathing, and the smell of midnight dew settling on the cold grass. Mr. Knox's eyes were closed; he looked so peaceful, beautiful lying in the tall green grass; no clothes, no cares, just us together. It was perfection. I gently pulled myself off his chest and started gathering and putting my clothes back on. By the time he had noticed I was almost fully clothed; I threw him his pants and told him we had to get going. It was getting late and we both had to sneak back into our houses. He sat up but that was it, he didn't want to move, not yet so he stayed in the grass and watched me collect myself. I finished buttoning my shirt then I knelt down to give him a kiss, he tried to get me back on the ground with him but I knew once would be enough for tonight and I walked away leaving him naked in the cold grass.

I felt like I was on air, I would never forget that night. I wanted to remember everything; every touch, every kiss, the way he felt, tasted, the way his lips felt on my skin. They say you never forget your first, well I do believe that to be true.

Once out of Mr. Knox's line of vision I started to run, I didn't want my rush to end. It was nearly one in the morning by the time I had snuck back into the house. I didn't go to bed, couldn't sleep; instead I went up to my haven and replayed the night over and over again in my mind until sleep finally took me. The alarm woke me after what felt like twenty minutes but was actually five hours later and I could feel it. My high was gone which was disappointing; I was excited and fearful to go to school; excited to see Mr. Knox but afraid to see him at the same time. How would he treat me now? And David, what about David? Would he know? Figure it out? He was always good at reading me. Could I hide this from him?"

Chapter Nine: Desire

Gabriella stopped for a moment to see if Dr. Wiseman was going to react to all she had said. She could see he was processing it and after a quick second, Gabriella realized he wasn't going to say anything yet so she carried on with her story.

"As I got ready for school and to meet David, I couldn't get the night before out of my mind. I wanted it to be night again so I could be with Mr. Knox, feel his touch. I made it through breakfast at the diner with David without him noticing my changed state, though it took all my concentration not to give anything away but I was glad I was able to keep my secret.

We had a double class of English and I was eager; when I got there, Mr. Knox and David were already there; David sitting in his seat while Mr. Knox was at his desk marking someone's homework. When I came in they both looked up and smiled, David stood up and hugged me and I could feel Mr. Knox's eyes on us. I wanted to speak to him but I had to be careful in front of David so when I turned to speak to Mr. Knox, I simply said hi and asked what we were doing in class today. Mr. Knox smiled; I could tell he was being careful too with David sitting there.

"Actually I have a really cool assignment for today." he looked so cute trying to contain his excitement.

"Cool" that's all I could say to him and I felt so lame saying it; Mr. Knox was still smiling and gazing at me. I found it hard to concentrate on anything else. After a moment or two, David turned to Mr. Knox

71

and said, "What's wrong with you? You get some really good news or something?"

"Yeah, I got really good news last night; guess I'm still taking it in."

David could see the small grin on my face and Mr. Knox's as Mr. Knox gazed back my way.

"Right" was all he said before turning back in his seat choosing to ignore the unsubtle looks between Mr. Knox and me. The rest of the class filed in as the bell went.

"Right" Mr. Knox started off the class, moving to the front of the room; I had never seen him so enthused to give us an assignment but then I doubted it was really the assignment that was making him so happy.

"Today we're going to do something that well, I think is fun. As you all know we've been studying poetry, different styles, different poets, well today I want you to be the poet. I want you to write a poem." He looked around the classroom watching most of his students look less than enthused with his assignment.

"So since we have a double block today I'm giving you the entire class to research the type of poem you wish to write and then of course to write it. Now for those of you who might be a bit more artistic" Mr. Knox looked right at me as he said this, "and seeing how once they're done I'm going to make you all present your poems in front of everyone anyway, you may come up with a more entertaining way to present your poem." That seemed to get everyone more on board with his assignment. "So go, I want you all to head down to the library and work, create something meaningful to you and come up with a unique way of presenting it to everyone. I will be down in a few minutes" He watched as the whole class started to gather their things and file out of the classroom down to the library. I kept my eyes on Mr. Knox as he silently told me to stay. David nudged me to get my attention. I told him I had to speak with Mr. Knox about a different assignment and that I would follow in a minute. David huffed a bit as he picked up his books and followed the rest of our classmates out leaving Mr. Knox and I alone.

I moved to sit atop my desk as Mr. Knox closed and locked the classroom door before moving to stand before me. Leaning into me placing his hands at my side on the desk I could feel his breath on my skin as my heart started to beat faster. He quickly glanced over to the door before fully embracing me and kissing me deeply. I let his tongue explore my mouth again and softly moaned as that burning desire started to rise in the pit of my stomach again. Memories of the night before flooded my mind and I wanted him to take me right there on my desk. I wrapped my arms around him as our kiss deepened and I could feel his arousal through his jeans. We broke apart simply for the necessity of air.

"God I want you" he breathed as he gently nibbled my earlobe. I had to bit my lower lip just to stay quiet. He was being reckless, we both were; it was the middle of the school day where anyone could see us. He kissed me hungrily again as his eyes filled with anticipating lust and desire.

"Tonight?" I pant out after his devious kiss.

"Yes" Mr. Knox groaned with a slight chuckle "if you can last that long" he smirked at me and I had to fight the urge to smack him for his playfulness. Instead, I leaned in close only to whisper:

"Can you?" placing a kiss on his cheek I moved off my desk, grabbed my books and headed for the door to join my classmates in the library. I looked back to him giving him my best coy smile before heading out the door.

Mr. Knox came into the library a few minutes after I had. I was already sitting next to David when he came up to us and quietly said, "You should sing" he spoke just loud enough for David to hear, smirking as he walked away leaving us to our work.

"How does he know you sing?" David inquired curiously but instead I ignored his question and asked him what kind of poem he was going to write.

Mr. Knox had given us until the next day to write our poems. I had given a lot of thought to his suggestion of singing. During our double block and for the rest of the day really I thought about Mr. Knox and myself, David and myself, what I had done.

That night when I left Mr. Knox in the room he had booked at the local Inn, I tried to work through everything that was happening in my life but my thoughts continually came back to Mr. Knox. With everything swarming in my mind, I meant to write a poem but it turned into a song. It wasn't until class the next day when I really made up my mind;

I had bought my guitar in case I chose to play. Everyone was excited to see what their classmates had come up with while I was more curious to see what David had written.

Mr. Knox started the class same as always then he started choosing people to come up and share their poems. No one had gotten all that creative with their poems; and for the most part they weren't all bad. Most wrote about graduation, parties, their boyfriend or girlfriend. I could tell Mr. Knox was saving me for last; I didn't mind so much but when he called David up, I got excited. I could tell David was nervous, he wasn't much of a public speaker but he pulled himself through it.

"I've um... done a free verse poem so... here it goes...

> *I was never one for words,*
> *But you were,*
> *I learnt to love them as you did,*
> *My life was empty till you came around*
> *My heart was lonely*
> *Till you heard my cry*
> *You never changed me,*
> *But took me as I was*
> *We've laughed, we've cried,*
> *We've held each other close*
> *I don't think you know*
> *How important you are*
> *You've been through hell*
> *So we take things slow*
> *But let me tell you now*
> *How you're the world to me*
> *And how I love you so."*

David's poem was beautiful and I found myself looking back and forth between him and Mr. Knox. As David sat back down I leaned over to him telling him how much I enjoyed his poem but I could see the discomfort on Mr. Knox's face. He figured the poem was meant for me and I had the same thought, something else I'd have to deal with down the line. Mr. Knox called me up next, with a hopeful look on his face. I could tell he hoped my poem would relate to him in some way. I stood and grabbed my guitar, I figured why not; I took my place at the front and started.

"My poem turned into a song while I was writing it… so yeah…" after my eight bar intro I started to sing.

"I don't know, where I stand
I don't know, where I am
And I don't know, what to do
I don't know, I don't know oh

Can I run, from this place?
Can I flee, from despair?
Will I forever feel this empty?
This cold

I don't know, how to shed my shame
I don't know, how to rid my burdens
And I don't know, how to be on my own
I don't know, I don't know oh

Can I run, from this place?
Can I flee, from despair?
Will I forever feel this empty?
This cold

And if I surrender all my pains
Will they all just wash away?
Can I be free, in you?
Or will I forever be?

I don't know, where I stand
I don't know, where I am
And I don't know, what to do
I don't know, I don't know."

I played my four bar outro to finish the slow pace melody then let my audience react.

I saw the looks of all my classmates, some had tears in their eyes, and some were just astonished. I was the quiet girl who didn't say much, they didn't expect anything like that from me, something so deep, meaningful and surreal all at the same time. I looked at Mr. Knox, he looked sad, my song had shown him another side of me, showed him just how much pain I was in. He almost looked ashamed, he knew my life, my past and he felt so deeply for me. I took my seat next to David, I could tell he wanted to say something, but couldn't find the words. The bell went and school was over. Mr. Knox grabbed me on the way out holding me back and waiting for everyone to leave before speaking.

"I... I had no idea," that's all he could say, I had caused him pain, he was changed by my song but I saw no other way of telling both him and David what I felt. David and I had become so distant and I wanted to try to tell him why, and with Mr. Knox and me getting closer; I just needed everyone to be on the same page and that song was the best way to do it. I let Mr. Knox continue to speak.

"Oh love, that was beautiful, and painful. I'm glad you chose to sing, I truly am," he paused for a second, "I had no idea just how much life had hurt you." I kissed him, I didn't care that we were in public, the classroom was empty; I kissed him."

Gabriella stopped talking again and stared at Dr. Wiseman, she had shared slightly more than she had intended to. He had been the very first person she told about sleeping with her teacher; Gabriella figured Dr. Wiseman must have processed that piece of information by now. As Gabriella thought about it, again she found herself wanting to laugh. Sleeping with your teacher, who actually does that? You see it in the movies, and read it in books but in reality you don't do it, you don't sleep with the very off-limits man. Gabriella never believed herself to be that type of person. Gabriella had always believed that she would be better off on her own; she certainly never wanted to end up like her parent's; a mother who killed herself and an abusive father who went insane. So this was Gabriella's choice, suicide or insanity? Some choice.

"Miss Harris, Gabriella, Gabs, Gabs, Are you alright?" as Dr. Wiseman called her name, you could hear the worry in his voice, "Gabriella."

Trying to grab her attention she puzzled him and he began to wonder if maybe he had taken on too large a challenge. *'No'* was the next through in his head, *'no, you can help her. She's lost so help her. Save her.'* The thoughts kept turning in his mind as he called Gabriella's name again trying to get her attention.

"Sorry, Dr. Wiseman lost in thought I guess."

"That's alright, what was the thought?"

"Just you're the first person I've told. You're the only one who knows, and well, the first time I've said it aloud actually. So I guess I just had to take all that in," Gabriella had this realized look on her face, almost like relief, she had finally told someone her secret and for the first time she wasn't afraid and that's what Dr. Wiseman saw in her expression. *'He's got her, Gabriella can see that what has happened is wrong on more than one level, perhaps if he could just get Gabriella away from Mr. Knox then maybe he could help her get her life back on track.'*

"Dr. Wiseman I think it's important for you to know that it wasn't just a onetime thing with Mr. Knox. We are still seeing each other actually... I sneak out of the house at night and meet him at the local inn, we've become quite good at sneaking around actually; hiding from everyone. I don't mean to say I enjoy lying to David and sneaking around him but at the same time I don't exactly want everyone to know that I'm seeing a married man... seeing my teacher..."

"So," Dr. Wiseman took advantage of Gabriella's pause, "what do you plan to do then?"

"Well... um... I'm just a couple of weeks away from graduating and my aunt and uncle want me to go to college and study history, English language, you see I love history and literature, of course, I read everything I can get my hands on. I was accepted into GreenBay College; you know that's actually the same college my parents and Mr. Knox attended, oddly enough. However, I don't know if that's what I want to do. I mean it's not far but I would only come home maybe once a month or less and with David and I on rocky terms these days. Mr. Knox and myself... I... well... I just don't know what to do. Mr. Knox told me he'd been searching for me for a long time. I'm not sure if I can believe such a line but he told me that after he heard about me, he wanted to know me, find me; but was never able to. I truly believe that... I mean after everything we've endured... I just; how do you walk away from someone when you've been through so much with them?"

Dr. Wiseman could see Gabriella's distrust. The decision she's trying to make was anything but simple, stay with the man she believes to be in love with or go away and live the life she deserves. Love or life? The hard questions and decisions at such a young age, in Dr. Wiseman's eye this was cruel and unfair; but he was curious about one thing involving Mr. Knox.

"Gabriella what are Mr. Knox's plans?" Gabriella just sat there with a blank look on her face.

"Plans, what do you mean by plans?" she asked after a minute.

"Well," Dr. Wiseman started to explain what he meant, "well, he is married, has a good job at the school and at the moment he also has you, so, I guess what I'm wondering is what he's planning to do about any of this? Is he going to leave his wife? Rearrange his life; for what you want or need? Or is he expecting you to simply stay here forever, stay with his wife and keep you on the side? Because let me tell you Gabs, you do not deserve that, you deserve to go to college, be happy, not be stuck in a relationship with a man who's done moving forward with his life. Have the two of you even discussed any of this?" Dr. Wiseman was waiting for Gabriella's reaction to everything, he wondered if she had even thought about any of it herself, or perhaps she was living the fantasy hoping never wake up. Gabriella just sat there and by the look on her face, Dr. Wiseman could see she had absolutely no idea.

"Well," Gabriella finally spoke but her voice was a bit shaky, "um... well... every time I try to bring up GreenBay he always seems to get me off the subject and we never actually talk about it."

Dr. Wiseman had his answer; Mr. Knox was not planning on having Gabriella's best interest at heart. How could he help Gabriella with this? How could he help her understand that even though he may be the love of her life; she might not be the love of his? As Dr. Wiseman watched Gabriella work this problem out in her head, he could see the light slowly turning on and it pained him to watch.

"Gabriella I really believe that you and Mr. Knox need to have an actual conversation and not allow him to dictate where it goes. Now tell me, what do you want to do? Stay here, or go off to college? Do you even know what you want?"

Gabriella was dumbstruck, what did she want? She had never actually thought about it. Before Mr. Knox, Gabriella had wanted to leave Babylon; she became so swept away by the intensity of him and since there meeting nothing else had really seemed to matter. Gabriella had rewritten her life to fit into his; she had stopped thinking past him; forgot to figure out what she wanted in life. After all wasn't that the reason she came to Dr. Wiseman in the first place, so she could hear the things that she had done out loud, see the mistakes she had made and to find a solution? Gabriella actually started to think about it. Her entire story now seemed so ridiculous; she had placed so much energy in her relationship with Mr. Knox and yes her relationship with him was completely wrong, he's her teacher, he's married, twice her age and for the most part given her heartache and lies. Gabriella never lied or kept secrets until Mr. Knox came into her life; and David, oh poor David, her closest friend who had been nothing but loving and devoted to her through their entire friendship. How could she be so cruel to her closest and only friend? Yes, she loved Mr. Knox that had not changed; she fell in love with him and she would always love him; however, she could not keep lying to everyone, to David or to herself.

Dr. Wiseman sat in silence watching Gabriella try to figure out what she was going to do, to decide on what she truly wanted as he watched her he noticed that Gabriella's eyes were venturing on and off the Bible, he had handed to her in their last session. Gabriella had left it there but Dr. Wiseman decided to leave it believing she would come back to it at some point. He thought that perhaps a slight nudge would do the trick.

"Gabriella, like I said in our last session, that book can be a great deal of help to you. God can help you but it will take a bit of trust and willingness to change. Now I'm not saying it's easy because believe me it's not; it's hard and challenging and in fact choosing the path of God is more likely to be a harder way of living than if you continue down the path you're on. That being said the path of God is a much better choice, yes hard and challenging but so much more rewarding than anything else you could choose..." as Dr. Wiseman tried to explain the benefits of God to Gabriella she picked up the Bible and started to flip through it.

"...So Gabriella, do you know what you want to do yet?" Dr. Wiseman asked after a few minutes; he was very hopeful at this moment, hoping Gabriella would end her affair with Mr. Knox, come clean to David, but above everything she would give God the chance he deserved. Gabriella was nodding her head up and down slowly.

"Tell me something, Dr. Wiseman, what do you think of my story?" Dr. Wiseman had foreseen this question. He had been thinking about how to answer it throughout this last session.

"Miss. Harris your life has not been an easy one, that's for sure. You have faced horrors in your childhood, your mother's suicide, your father's insanity; those are not easy things to deal with. I do believe that David is a great part of your life and I would come clean to him about everything. Now I am not telling you what to do, this is just what I would do personally. If I had someone as loyal and devoted to me, I would try to be very open and honest with that person. Now regarding Mr. Knox," he paused for a moment, "Mr. Knox has seduced you and chased you even when he knew better. Mr. Knox is the adult here and what he's done with you is anything but right. That said; you also need to take responsibility for your role in all of this. Now yes, Mr. Knox seduced you but you still made the choice to engage and encourage him. Even though your relationship with this man started as a friendship, which was unacceptable enough, and Mr. Knox knew that. It's quite like my profession, I cannot be friends and have an emotional bond with one of my patients, now yes there needs to be a level of trust as we had established at the beginning. However, our relationship could never go farther than what we have established. That being said I do care what happens to you and I want to help you make decisions that will cause you the least amount of pain. Do you understand? Our relationship is much like the one you and Mr. Knox were supposed to have; you two crossed the line when you both decided to move past the student/teacher creed, and a relationship like the one you are in is very unhealthy; especially for someone of your age," he finished.

Gabriella took a small moment before responding to Dr. Wiseman.

"So according to you I have to end my relationship with Mr. Knox; tell David everything that I've been keeping from him? That's basically what you're telling me here, Dr. Wiseman." Gabriella couldn't hide the tint of attitude in her voice as she spoke to him.

"Gabriella, please, let me make it clear that I'm not here to tell you what to do, what I'm telling you is, is that you need to decide what's best for you," Dr. Wiseman could see that Gabriella understood that. She was going to have to make some hard decisions but those decisions had to be hers. Gabriella will need to block out everything and listen to herself but more importantly, she needed to listen to her heart.

"I can't change how I feel about Mr. Knox, that I love him," Gabriella wanted to make that very clear.

"I know, Gabs, but that does not change the issue. Do you know how he feels about you? That's my question. Does he love you enough to put your best interest at heart, above his own wants and needs because if he doesn't and only wants you for his own selfish reasons, then how is that good for you? How does that give you what you need?" He paused to let Gabriella take everything in for a moment then continued, "Unfortunately, Gabriella, our time is up, how is this time next week for you? And I would like you to really think about everything we've talked about today. Secrets and lies is no way to live and I do believe that you are worth so much more than what you've gotten in life." Dr. Wiseman was unsettled by the way he was leaving their session, but his six o'clock patient was waiting for him.

"Ok," Gabriella replied in agreement. She gave Dr. Wiseman a half smile as she grabbed the Bible off the table and stood up from his couch.

"Thanks for listening, for the advice. I'll see you next week." And with that Gabriella walked out of Dr. Wiseman's office leaving him sitting in his chair to ponder everything Gabriella had told him; then he carried on with his next appointment.

Chapter Ten: Faith

Gabriella was more confused now than when she had first entered Dr. Wiseman's office; she replayed all her session with him repeatedly in her mind on her walk home. Dr. Wiseman's office was only a few blocks away from where Gabriella lived but she wasn't ready to go home quite yet, so she decided to go to the abandoned park and think a while, with the Bible still in her hands she set off for the park.

Once Gabriella was at the park, she sat down on the swing-set and started to sway a bit while skimming through the Bible.

'God, really? How is God supposed to help?' Gabriella couldn't see how an invisible entity was going to solve all her problems. She dropped the Bible on the ground and started to swing herself a bit harder. As Gabriella looked around the abandoned park she remembered the first night she found the park; empty and quiet it had become her second favourite place to go outside of her haven. Gabriella hadn't told anyone that she loved to go swing at the old park; no one until Mr. Knox. As Gabriella started to swing higher and higher she remember the night she had Mr. Knox meet her in the park; it was one of the best nights of her life; the most unexpected. Gabriella remembered everything about that night; while they were lying on the cold tall uncut grass Mr. Knox had asked why she chose the park; how when she said because it's beautiful the look of surprise on Mr. Knox's glowing face. Gabriella remembered him taking a moment to view his surroundings only to turn back to her

and say "You're right; I can't believe I never saw it before" smile and kiss her again.

As Gabriella swung higher, she kept trying to find her peace. That quiet place in her mind where she could make sense of the world around her, but she couldn't get there.

"Tell David? Leave Mr. Knox? College? Stay in Babylon? God?" The thoughts swarmed her mind like a parasite, never ending, completely consuming. Gabriella thought of everything that had happened between herself and Mr. Knox; every night spent together, every hidden kiss, it was passionate; they were passionate and exhilarating. Gabriella thought of the start of their acquaintance; they did nothing but talk about Alice her mother; Mr. Knox's days with her. That's how everything started, but their acquaintance turned into friendship, which turned into lovers. Gabriella had begun to notice once they became lovers everything changed, the conversations started to dwindle while the passion they shared only increased. Every time Gabriella and Mr. Knox would start a conversation their lust, would consume them and take over.

'Was this it?' Gabriella thought, *'was this the best of our relationship? Could we never go back to the long intriguing talks? Spending time together, which didn't extend past sex? I always loved our long intellectual conversations but was that finished now? Would it only ever be about sex at this point?'* Gabriella started to lose track of each individual thought and it started to hurt. She decided that perhaps it was time to call it a night and head home; she jumped off the swing, grabbed the Bible and set off home.

Gabriella was determined to solve at least some of her problems; her aunt had taken to leaving little non-subtle hints about GreenBay every time they spoke. The next morning Gabriella's mind still hadn't settled down but she had decided to, at least sort out the whole Mr. Knox relationship thing before even considering college or anything else. She was nervous, not sure if she could even face Mr. Knox or David; she thought about what Dr. Wiseman told her about lies and secrets, how unhealthy of a life she was living. Gabriella knew that she couldn't think about these things forever. She glanced over to the Bible sitting on top of her dresser, as she got ready for school. *'Maybe'* Gabriella thought as she stared over at the Bible, *'maybe he's right? Maybe God?'* Another thing

Gabriella couldn't take forever to think about. She left ready and heading for school but she found the closer she got the greater feeling of dread grew stronger in the pit of her stomach. 'No,' she thought, 'not today.' Therefore, instead of turning down Drover Street, which would take her to school Gabriella kept walking straight down Elk Street until she got to the bus stop; then she waited.

Gabriella wasn't entirely sure what she was going to do but she thought that perhaps spending the day away from everything would help clear her head.

Gabriella found the bus exhilarating, the idea that she could simply get on and go anywhere was freeing. She had imagined leaving the little town of Babylon so many times but never actually had the courage to go. Gabriella thought of her trip to Europe with David and how she felt; she thought of going back to Rome or Paris, maybe even seeing something new. Gabriella dreamt of being anywhere but Babylon, far away from her problems; but for the day she decided to go just one town over: Riverton.

When the bus arrived in Riverton, Gabriella departed and just set off in the first direction she came too. No idea as to where she was heading and she didn't care. She just wanted to see something different, to see what was in the town. Riverton was small like Babylon but they had so much more. As Gabriella walked up and down every little street she could find, she noticed that her mind was actually starting to settle down. She watched everyone around her, the people sitting outside cafe's having coffee, kids coming out of the sweet shop with their parents holding small bags of candy. Gabriella felt like she walked into a scene from one of her books. Riverton seemed to have everything from malls and coffee shops to an amusement park. This was exactly what Gabriella wanted and needed an entire town to distract her.

The day seemed to go by far too quickly, before Gabriella knew it she was waiting for the bus back to Babylon. Gabriella loved every minute of her day of rebellion; she did everything; rode the rides and played the park games, had coffee that cost way too much and wandered the Riverton Mall; watched the people around her live their lives the way normal healthy everyday people do. The day out of Babylon, away from everything and everyone did Gabriella a world of good, just as she had hoped it would. Gabriella finally has a quiet mind for the first time in months; and she finally knew what she wanted.

It was around nine at night when Gabriella finally walked in the front door of her house. Aunt Enid, as Gabriella predicted, was pacing up and down the kitchen going out of her mind while Uncle John just sat at the table reading the evening paper. Once Enid saw Gabriella leaning against the kitchen door she started to go off on her.

"Where the **HELL** have you been? The school called, you never showed up, your teacher Mr. Knox kept calling and he showed up here; David too. What were you thinking just going off like that? Not telling anyone. Where have you been all day then?" John finally looked up from his paper to his wife's last question waiting to hear Gabriella's answer while his wife continued to pace and pant from all her yelling. Gabriella ignored her aunt directing her response to John.

"I went up to Riverton today. It was great and I had fun." Gabriella and her uncle shared a smile then John went back to his paper; Gabriella knew that despite her aunt going off the handle that it was fine.

"**RIVERTON? WHAT? WHY? WHAT THE HELL HAS GOTTEN INTO THAT HEAD OF YOURS? THIS IS NOT OKAY...**" Enid went on and on while Gabriella sat down across from her uncle and started reading the parts of the paper he was done with. Once Gabriella finished reading the paper and Enid ran out of things to yell about, she left her aunt and uncle in the kitchen and headed up to her room. David was sitting on Gabriella's bed when she walked in and turned the light on.

"Gabs," she jumped at the sound of his voice; not anticipating it.

"What... how did you get in here?" she asked while regaining her senses.

"Your bedroom window, Gabs where the hell have you been all day?" Gabriella could see David's anger and knew she had to explain herself.

"David, look... I'm sorry I disappeared today but I... I just needed some space. Time to think, I've had a lot on my mind lately," Gabriella knew that line wouldn't work on him but she couldn't think of anything else to say.

"You're sorry; you've had a lot on your mind lately? Really? What do you think has been going through my mind lately? What's going on between you and Mr. Knox?" David was wasting no time, "I've seen the looks between you two so you tell me, you tell me right now Gabs, what's been going on?"

Gabriella had never seen David so angry before, she had really hurt him and she never meant for that. He was standing in front of her now waiting for her to answer him.

"Okay, okay David, but you have to stay calm, and hear me out." Gabriella paused while David sat back down on the bed agreeing to stay calm and hear her out. "Mr. Knox and I... we've been seeing each other for the past few months... we're lovers David and I didn't want to tell you... you could barely handle things when Mr. Knox and I were just friends..."

David started to laugh; he was in shock. Not because he was surprised by, what Gabriella was telling him, because all his suspicions about her and Mr. Knox were right. He was shaking his head as he began to speak.

"I knew it, I just... I knew it and since when have the two of you ever been 'just friends'? Since that very first day in class when we met him, there's been this... this connection between you and it was not just because of your mother. No, oh no Gabs, you and Mr. Knox have never been 'just friends'."

Gabriella stood in front of David, completely frozen. He was right and she knew it. She and Mr. Knox had never been 'just friends'; David had said it, that first day in class there was that immediate connection between them. Gabriella really didn't know what to say at this point.

"Why do you even care so much, David? It's not like it's any of your business." The moment the words came out of her mouth Gabriella regretted it and by the look on David's face, he couldn't believe what she had said. He was even angrier now and was ready to walk away. He had had enough. David shook his head, stood up off the bed and headed for the door; just before walking out he turned to Gabriella and said, "You are so blind, Gabriella Harris, so freaking blind."

Then he was gone.

Chapter Eleven: Conflict

The next couple of days were bad; David still wasn't talking to Gabriella and she had yet to resolve anything with Mr. Knox. Gabriella wasn't sure how much longer she could avoid the conversation she knew needed to happen. She could only hope that David would forgive her one day and that Mr. Knox would understand. Gabriella decided to sort everything out with Mr. Knox before anything else, and then she'd try to smooth things out with David again. When Gabriella got a free moment from her aunt and uncle, she headed to her room to call Mr. Knox. Gabriella was not thrilled when his wife, Grace, picked up the phone but luckily, she and Mr. Knox had created a system for when this happened. Once Grace said hello, Gabriella would ask for someone else, Grace would say 'sorry wrong number' and Mr. Knox would know to call Gabriella back.

Mr. Knox was glad to hear from Gabriella, it had been a few days and he hated that.

"Gabs, love where have you been? I've been worried," Mr. Knox, asked the same question everyone was and now she'd have to answer them for a third time. Instead of giving him the answers he wanted Gabriella told Mr. Knox that she needed to see him as soon as possible. Mr. Knox was always more than happy to meet her so by the end of their phone call they had agreed to meet at the local inn a little after ten. At ten when Gabriella heard her aunt and uncle go to bed, she snuck out her bedroom window and headed off to the local Babylon Inn.

The inn was only a twenty minute walk; Mr. Knox was already there waiting outside the office door. Gabriella felt herself beginning to melt. She could feel herself fall farther with every step toward him. She loved him, how could she not? Gabriella had given Mr. Knox every part of her; she had never hidden a single thing from him, never lied or withheld anything. He was her first love, first lover; Gabriella felt closer to him than anyone else; and she didn't want any of it to end. The closer she got to Mr. Knox the more handsome he became, she had forgotten over the last few days just how alluring she found him to be. Gabriella was convinced that what Mr. Knox and herself shared was love and not simply lust as Dr. Wiseman had implied. *'He must love me too,'* was the only thought running through Gabriella's mind.

When Gabriella reached Mr. Knox, she went to speak but before she could say anything, he grabbed her roughly and kissed her passionately. No waiting, no hiding, it was an out in the open everything goes kiss. Gabriella couldn't help herself, as much as she knew she should resist him she couldn't. She stopped caring and decided to let go of everything else and fall into his grasp. Gabriella embraced Mr. Knox just as vigorously as he had her. They were hopeless, too much passion, too much lust, love, trust. Gabriella was convinced he was it, the one, no one else would do. Gabriella needed to focus, there was a reason for their meeting and it was not this, but it was beginning to be a very close second in Gabriella's mind and a definite first in Mr. Knox's.

Finding the will Gabriella gently pushed herself, breaking away from Mr. Knox.

"Did you get a room?" Gabriella wanted to talk but she asked so soft and sweetly she couldn't resist. Mr. Knox simply held up the room key and smiled; he took Gabriella by the hand and led her up the stairs to their room. Gabriella knew what Mr. Knox was thinking; she only hoped she would have the courage to say what needed to be said before things went any further.

Mr. Knox opened the door and headed in while Gabriella stood frozen in the doorway. Mr. Knox noticed as he loosened his tie.

"Gabs, love, what is it? What's the matter? Come on love I guarantee it's much better in here than standing in the doorway! Gabs... love...?" he was becoming concerned as he watched Gabriella stand frozen in the doorway. Mr. Knox walked over to her, placed one hand around her waist and took her hand with his other then gently pulled her into the room closing the door behind them.

The room had a very pleasant feel to it, light beige painted walls with dark hardwood floors with a cute circled red carpet in the centre of the room, queen size bed covered in blood red sheets, a tall cabinet across from the bed containing a TV and a mini fridge next to it. Mr. Knox wrapped his other hand around Gabriella's waist holding her close to his body; they stood swaying in each other's arms back and forth, noses almost touching. Mr. Knox had started to kiss Gabriella starting at her forehead and slowly working his way down just shy of her shoulders, then moving back up her neck up to her cheek.

"We... we really need to talk," Gabriella had finally managed to squeeze the words out in between each kiss. Mr. Knox stopped kissing her and backed a couple of steps away from her nodding in agreement.

"I know, love, I know," he replied.

"Okay, good," Gabriella went and at down on the bed, she was finally getting what she needed, while Mr. Knox stood right where he was but turned to face Gabriella on the bed.

"Look..." Gabriella started but Mr. Knox interrupted her before she could get any farther.

"Gabs, love, I can't do this anymore." You could see the relief explode from his face as he managed to get the words out in the open. Gabriella was surprised and went to speak again but Mr. Knox still wouldn't let her.

"Love I can't do this, all this sneaking around, lying to Grace, I've decided that I'm done," Mr. Knox took a breath before finishing the rest of his spiel, "Love, I'm leaving Grace." There was a pause in the room. Neither could speak. Mr. Knox was waiting for Gabriella's reaction but she couldn't give him one, she was in shock. He had said the words she never believed him capable yet always secretly wished he would. After another few awkward silent second Mr. Knox continued.

"I cannot be with her when all I think about is you. I want you love, no one else. I... I love you Gabriella Harris and I don't want to love anybody else." Mr. Knox moved to sit next to her on the bed, he had shocked her, but he had also said the one thing she needed him to say.

Gabriella was dumbstruck, and Mr. Knox could see it; it was definitely not what she was expecting from him. He shuffled closer and closer to Gabriella taking both her hands in his as he stared into her wide hazel eyes. He was waiting for her to say something, anything, but she couldn't find the words.

"Gabs, Gabs, love, please, say something here, anything?" Mr. Knox was desperate not to be hanging out there with an 'I love you' caught in the middle. He had a firm yet gentle grip on Gabriella's hands waiting for her to say or do anything that showed him that she heard him after a moment or two Gabriella had managed to find her voice.

"You... um... sorry but... you love me? And... and you're leaving your wife... and... and..." Gabriella fell silent again.

"Yes," was all Mr. Knox said but it seemed to be enough. Gabriella without saying another word leaned in and kissed him. They went slow and gentle, like their first night together; except this was different; sad yet embracing. They both knew that after tonight everything was going to be different. They could sense the change in each other; they simply weren't sure if that change was for the better or worse. Their passion once again had consumed them. Mr. Knox must have kissed Gabriella a thousand times before starting to unbutton her blouse and even still he never stopped kissing her, her cheek, her neck, moving slowly down while his hands were working on each button. He shifted her onto her back as Gabriella started to pull at his shirt. The shirt and blouse were the first to end up on the floor, followed by the socks and shoes, stroking and kissing each other every step of the way but eventually their ardour took over entirely, it was perfect, everything was perfect and right, every moment, every hand placement, it really was the best either had had together. Mr. Knox couldn't help but admire the young beauty beneath him as he deeply kissed her once more. Neither of them wanted it to end; they just wanted to lay there forever consumed by each other; but they knew that even though their love was great, they couldn't go on forever. Gabriella realized that in spite of everything she still hadn't told Mr. Knox she loved him.

Mr. Knox was lying next to Gabriella gazing at her, running his fingers up and down her arm. Gabriella was staring up at the ceiling holding back the tears that were swelling in her eyes. Without a moment's hesitation Gabriella turned her head toward Mr. Knox and said, "I love you."

But Mr. Knox already knew that, he leaned in to kiss her again before she could say anything else, "I know you do, love, I know you do."

Mr. Knox didn't understand Gabriella's desire to say the words; she needed to make him understand so she turned on her side to face Mr. Knox and tried again, "No, I love you, I love you so much and because of how much I love you, it just makes this all the more harder to say."

Gabriella paused for a second to collect her thoughts while examining the confused expression on Mr. Knox's face, "I... I got into GreenBay College and... well... well I've decided to go which means... well... um... which means..." Gabriella could see all the happiness fall from Mr. Knox's perfect face.

"You're leaving," he closed his eyes as the words fell from his lips.

"Yes, it's a four year program... not sure how often I'd come home, come back to Babylon..." Mr. Knox stopped her again.

"So what does this mean for us then? I can't go back to Grace, I won't go back and I don't want to be without you," he had such a look of desperation on his face.

"I don't know." the tears in Gabriella's eyes started to fall now and Mr. Knox caught them with his fingers.

"We can work this out, can't we love?" he was not only trying to comfort Gabriella but himself. He didn't want Gabriella to leave but he knew he could not stand in the way of her experiencing something as great as college. He kissed her again because this time he knew they were limited.

"Look, this doesn't necessarily mean goodbye, graduation is next week and then it's summer and we could have the beginning together before I have to prepare for GreenBay; not sure just how much time we'd have but I'm sure there will be a moment or two, a night or so we can steal away." As soon as Gabriella said it, she realized that she was heartbroken. *This must be what a broken heart feels like,* she thought; from the look on Mr. Knox's face, Gabriella's heart wasn't the only one breaking. He had just lost the second woman he ever truly loved. First Gabriella's mother, Alice, and now her; it was clear to him how this would end, she needed to go off to college and he could not hold her back from experiencing all the things life had to offer.

"So," Mr. Knox started to speak as he pulled Gabriella closer to himself again, "this could very well be our last night together."

"There is a good chance of that, yes," Gabriella couldn't contain her tears anymore, the thought that she would never be with him again, especially now, now that he chose to leave his wife, confess his love, willing to throw everything away for her. It hurt.

"Look, I... I don't think you should leave Grace. I mean she is your wife and there's no reason..." but Gabriella couldn't finish her sentence.

"No, no," Mr. Knox was shaking his head, "no, it's over between Grace and I; I'm leaving her; so go off to college, live, enjoy and just maybe, God willing, you'll find your way back to me someday. I really do love you, Gabriella, and I want the world for you."

Tears were really falling down Gabriella's cheeks as Mr. Knox's words touched her. Then out of nowhere, Gabriella found herself wanting to ask Mr. Knox a very personal question.

"Do you believe in God?" the question just sort of slipped out of her and as she asked it; Gabriella realized that oddly enough God and their beliefs were the one subject they had never actually talked about. Mr. Knox kissed Gabriella gently and whispered, "Yes, I believe he sent me you." And that was it; there was nothing left to say. Everything had already been said and they were left with nothing but each other and the rest of the night.

Chapter Twelve: Decisions

Gabriella left Mr. Knox at the inn; she wandered the streets in the early morning remembering every moment she had ever spent with Mr. Knox. Gabriella snuck back through her bedroom window and crawled into bed; she only had forty-five minutes until she needed to get up for school. She was excited and sad at the same time. All the exams were done and all the last minute assignments had been handed in so going to school at this point was really just a formality. It was only a half day so Gabriella really didn't mind going, and then she had her session with Dr. Wiseman.

At school Gabriella tried to get David alone to talk to him, tell him what she had done, that it was over with Mr. Knox but of course, the only time she got with him was in English class. It wasn't as awkward seeing Mr. Knox as she thought it would be, but David, David was anything but happy to be in the same room with either of them.

"David, David please will you just listen to me for a moment then I promise you won't ever have to speak to me again if that's what you want," Gabriella pleaded, trusting David would at least hear her out. He nodded his head telling her that she was free to speak.

"Look, David, I'm sorry for what happened, for lying to you. It was never my intention to hurt you... I've ended things with Mr. Knox... it's over," Gabriella paused for a moment, "David... I'm not blind... I know how you feel about me... and I love you... I do love you just... I just can't love you the way you want me to, the way you love me." Gabriella stopped to let David take everything in and from the look on his face; he knew she was right.

David was in love with Gabriella and wanted her, the way Mr. Knox had her. It was the reason David and Mr. Knox never got along; they were both jealous of each other, wanting the same woman; it was worse for David because unlike Mr. Knox he never got what he wanted, he never got Gabriella; her heart, her love. David's eyes closed as a tear dropped from one; the realization of never having Gabriella as more than a friend hurt him.

"David, you need to know that I've been accepted into GreenBay College and well... I'm going. It's all been settled so that's it, I'm going and that's it, that's everything," Gabriella had said everything she wanted to and she waited for David response. After a few seconds David finally spoke.

"You're leaving. You're just going to leave, just like that?" David was not taking the news well.

"David it's time, I can't stay here anymore. I need to move on and find something new. I need to start living my life. You know you could try it yourself; change isn't all bad." Gabriella tried to smile as she said this; she really wanted David to understand where she was coming from.

"Yeah, right, well, have a good life then Gabriella Harris." David had this 'I'm sorry for being jerk, hope you'll be happy' look on his face. He was happy for her, he was just too hurt to play the 'yay you' role. He gave her a small smile telling her to stay safe, then he stood from his seat and headed for the classroom door. Just before leaving, David turned to face Mr. Knox who had taken notice of his departure. David gave him a slight head nod then walked away. Gabriella understood that David needed time and hoped that one day they could be as they were again.

Gabriella glanced over to Mr. Knox and he knew, she had told David everything; that everything would be all right in time. The bell rang and school was finished; the classroom emptied leaving Gabriella and Mr. Knox alone. Gabriella walked up to Mr. Knox, took his hands in hers and as if she was creating a final memory she whispered, "I love you; I'll miss you." And that was all she said. Gabriella gave him a gentle kiss, Mr. Knox not wanting to break from her pressed himself into her deepening their kiss and Gabriella let him. After a moment, Gabriella broke the kiss,

"I will always love you," she breathed as she dropped his hands, and walked out without a glance back.

Chapter Thirteen: Choices

Gabriella sat once again in Dr. Wiseman's small dull waiting room but this time it seemed different for her. There were no more arguments going on inside her head, she wasn't distracted by anything; for the first time for as long as Gabriella could remember there was nothing wrong, nothing to worry about. Gabriella felt calm and content, she dared to believe that she was almost happy, it was a feeling she wasn't sure how to process, but she didn't want it to go away either. As Gabriella sat in the small waiting room admiring her favourite photograph, the waterfall with its hidden face, she wasn't confused by it anymore but felt she almost understood it, understood who the face was. Gabriella was still admiring the photo when Dr. Wiseman opened his office door inviting her in.

Dr. Wiseman was happy to see Gabriella again; he had been worrying and praying, thinking about her all week. Gabriella stood up out from his hard wooden chair in his waiting room and walked straight into his office taking her seat on his cushy couch. Once Dr. Wiseman settled in his chair and started their session.

"So, how are you? Was your week all right? Any thought about what we talked about last week?" he wanted to know what Gabriella had decided, hoping his words to her during their last session had had some impact on her; even if only a little.

"Um, my week was good, hard and a bit hectic but good. I did a lot of thinking and made what I think to be the right decision." Dr. Wiseman smiled, truly hoping she had in fact made as she said, the right decision.

"Alright, tell me about it then. Tell me what you did this week, Gabriella." Dr. Wiseman was excited now.

"Well, I came clean to David, and well, he's not happy and needs time but I think he'll be alright after a while; I just don't know how long that while will be. So for now we've gone our separate ways, which as hard as that is it's good for now, we're just in two very different places right now." Dr. Wiseman stopped her there for a minute and asked, "What does David want?"

"He wants to stay right where he is, open a garage, he's always wanted to be a mechanic; and I think that's great, however he wanted me to stay here, with him; he wanted us to be together.' Dr. Wiseman smiled as this piece of information.

"I thought so," He said.

Gabriella looked puzzled by his comment so he explained it to her.

"Gabriella from what you've told me about David I got the impression he might have been in love with you, but I think that deep down inside somewhere you already knew that, and that's why you had such a hard time telling him about you and Mr. Knox. Am I right?" he could see that he was, "Tell me what else happened this week." Dr. Wiseman wanted to move on and not let her get lost in thoughts of David.

"Well, I had that well needed conversation with Mr. Knox. He told me that he loves me and that well... that he's leaving his wife." Gabriella paused to await Dr. Wiseman's expression and if he was going to say anything, a simple "and" was all she got.

"Well, as happy I was to hear all that I ended things with him. Actually, I told him I was leaving Babylon and going to GreenBay. So lots of change this week but I think everything's turning out for the best." Gabriella was smiling; Dr. Wiseman could see a great difference in her. He realized that all she needed was to tell someone her secrets too. Dr. Wiseman smiled and said, "Good for you Gabriella, it sounds like you've really turned things around for yourself."

"Yeah I guess I have," Gabriella replied, smiling.

Dr. Wiseman could see a great sign of relief lift from Gabriella; she looked as though all the baggage that had been holding her down had finally been lifted, but though all of this Dr. Wiseman sensed she had more to share so he asked her what else there was.

"You know, it's thanks to you really, you gave me that Bible and well, l read it. l think l understand the appeal of God. l asked Mr. Knox his beliefs, if he believed in God and you know what?" Dr. Wiseman shook his head no as Gabriella continued, "he believes God sent him me; l found that sweet, not sure if l believe it but I'm willing to take my chances. l think God just might be a road I'm willing to go down." Gabriella was happy; she felt as though her life was finally going in the right direction.

Dr. Wiseman couldn't believe what he was hearing; he was amazed by how quickly this train wreck of a young woman had completely turned her life around. Gabriella had been this young confused woman having an affair, lying to everyone, to herself, now she had given up the man she loved, stopped the affair, stopped lying to David and herself, chosen to attend college and found the Lord. Dr. Wiseman knew that Gabriella had a very long way to go but at least she was now heading in the right direction.

"Dr. Wiseman?" Gabriella had just one more thing to say to him before the end of their session.

"Yes, Gabriella?"

"l just wanted to thank you. You've helped me see my options, the choices l needed to make. This is how l see things. l had three roads l could choose from; the first road was to continue to stay on the road l was one, stay having an affair with Mr. Knox. The second road l could have left Mr. Knox, gotten together with David and he would have been happy, but l think that road would have left me with an emptiness; always having this feeling that l was missing something. l think l could have been happy with David, but l would have this sadness in me, which would one day probably consume me. Hmmm, maybe that's what happened to my mother. The third road, the one l chose; walk away, walk away from David, from Mr. Knox, and thanks to you walk toward God; find out what's out there for me and learn just what God has planned. Maybe one day when I'm all 'grown up' l could find myself with Mr. Knox or David, or perhaps someone else entirely down the road and just be happy and joyful in the life I've chosen to live."

Dr. Wiseman was proud, proud at how quickly Gabriella had figured out how the life she'd been living was not healthy, and that there was so much more out in the world somewhere waiting for her to find it. Furthermore he was proud at the fact Gabriella was willing to give God a chance and let him lead her. He felt he had followed God's wishes regarding Gabriella; he was able to save a young woman simply by trusting in God and keeping his faith strong.

Gabriella stood up from Dr. Wiseman's couch; she had said everything she had wanted to. Gabriella had gotten far more than she had ever expected or imagined by coming to see Dr. Wiseman, and she was happy she had finally let her guard down enough and let someone help her.

"Thank you for listening to my crazy story, making sense of it and not judging me for the choices and mistakes I've made," Gabriella stretched out her hand and waited for Dr. Wiseman to take it. He rose from his chair shaking her hand.

"You are more than welcome Miss. Harris, and I hope you know that my door is always open to you, anytime." They dropped hands and headed toward the door.

When they reached the door it looked as if Gabriella had something else to say but decided against it, she smiled as she turned away from Dr. Wiseman leaving his office.

When Gabriella got home she found that her aunt and uncle had gotten her a cheap little car, they told her it was so no matter what she could always come home again.

The summer went by quickly and before Gabriella knew it she was days away from starting at GreenBay College. The day Gabriella was leaving for school she received a final letter.

My dearest Gabriella,

I just wanted you to know that I do not regret anything that happened between us. I am fully divorced now and if it's all right with you, I'd like us to keep in touch while you're off at college. I love you and miss you greatly but I cannot and will not stand in your way. I refuse to hold you back form learning and living the life you so desperately deserve.

I remember the first day I saw you; I thought you were your mother, you look just like her and I'm sorry to say that for the longest time I wanted you in hopes of being with her again. I never did stop loving your mother and I don't think I ever could, however I found that I love you in ways I could never have loved her and I hope one day you'll forgive me for that; for trying to have a relationship with your mother through you.

I want you to know that you have my heart and soul, that I will forever be yours. I meant what I said to you; I will always wait for you because you are worth waiting for. I cannot see myself with anyone but you. I've been lucky in finding love twice in my life; but I do believe that you are my deepest and greatest love. I understand if you don't feel the same and I am more than happy simply remembering the times we shared together. Nothing will ever change my love for you. Please enjoy college, it really is the best years a person can have! I hope you can fully enjoy and appreciate everything you find there, I know I did.

I want you to know I will always cherish the gifts and time you have given me, I truly believe that you gave me the very best of yourself. In my eyes, you are perfect. Please remember that no matter what happens, don't ever change who you are; and know that there is someone in the world who loves you. So like I said you forever have my heart. I hope I have yours. Good luck love.

I love you
Aidan Edgar Knox

Gabriella had tears in her eyes as she read and re-read his letter. She was touched so deeply by his words and she knew he meant all of them. The contents of the letter did not surprise Gabriella, and she had long forgiven him concerning her mother. Gabriella knew exactly how he saw her; how it was her he truly loved. She also agreed with how she gave him the very best of herself. She gave him all that she was and that was something she could never regret, nor could she regret being with him. How could a person regret feeling such love? Gabriella considered what he had written, wondering if somewhere down the road, they could stay in touch; wondering if they could ever go back to what they were, the way they were. She wondered if she should. Eventually, doesn't everyone have to walk away from their first love? Or is it when you find that love you should hold on tight and never let go? Gabriella tucked the letter away and got ready to leave.

The car was fully loaded; Gabriella had a long drive ahead of her. Gabriella kissed her aunt and uncle goodbye, told them she'd be home for Christmas and not to worry, she thanked them for everything, taking her in, putting up with all her madness through the years but more importantly raising her, loving her as their own. Her uncle told her taking her in was the best decision they ever made. He told her how proud they were of her. Once the goodbyes were all said Gabriella climbed into her fully packed car, gave her aunt and uncle, the house and her bedroom window a final glance then drove off. Gabriella was scared and excited all at the same time. She was getting what she wanted.

Gabriella felt like she was breathing for the first time. Even though she was terrified, she was exhilarated. Finally, after everything, she had gone through; she was free. Gabriella had no idea what the road ahead had for her but she didn't mind, she wasn't sure if she'd ever really return to Babylon. If she'd ever see the ones she loves again, but none of that really seemed to matter anymore. Gabriella's fears no longer controlled her and she couldn't wait to see what was going to get thrown her way.

PART TWO: CONSEQUENCES

Chapter Fourteen: Change

As Gabriella sat at her desk starting blindly at her homework and all the studying she had to do for her finals; she could hardly believe how quickly the last four years had gone by and that she was now only two months away from graduating from GreenBay College. Gabriella was excited to be graduating from the same college that her parents Eli and Alice Harris and her formal lover Aidan Knox had all graduated from. Gabriella could remember a time when she wasn't even considering college and now here she was mere months away from being done.

Gabriella remembered how afraid she was those first few months at GreenBay, living in a new town knowing no one, being away from the family she had made back in Babylon. Her Aunt Enid and Uncle John; her friend David whom she hardly ever spoke to now and of course Aidan who even still corresponded with her from time to time. Gabriella even missed Dr. Wiseman, the one man who was truly able to help her figure out her life. Throughout Gabriella's first year at GreenBay College she would drive back to Babylon for every break, every holiday; but she found that as she started to make friends and build a life for herself that going home to Babylon became less and less of a priority.

Gabriella focused again on the essay she was trying to write for her English Lit class; she had to write on the similarities and differences between all of Jane Austen's novels; the heroines and heroes. English Lit was Gabriella's favorite class and certainty her favorite subject, she had been reading Austen's work for years now and knew them all imminently. As Gabriella got back on track her roommate Faith Mills opened her bedroom door and distracted her from her studies.

"Hey Gab's I'm heading out, just wanted to make sure we were still on for tonight?"

Gabriella shifted in her small black wheelie office chair to face Faith. "Yeah still good but ah why do we have to go out? What's wrong with just staying in?"

Faith just smiled as if she had a secret she couldn't share. "Trust me; you'll want to come out tonight." Faith smiled again; Gabriella knew she should just make her friend tell her what was going on; Faith had been acting odd for the last couple of days, odder than normal. So Gabriella knew that something was up but she was just too pre-occupied with all her studying to figure out whatever Faith had gone and done or dig out what secrets she was hiding.

Faith left Gabriella to her thoughts, leaving her door open. Gabriella shifted back to her essay but her mind wasn't there anymore, she was thinking about the past, how much she had changed since coming to GreenBay. Thinking of all the good that came from being there, she couldn't help but think of all the things she left behind.

Things still weren't great with David, Gabriella's first real friend and as much as she had tried to repair their friendship, she had to accept that they would never go back to the way things were. David simply could not forgive what he considered to be Gabriella's betrayal; for loving Mr. Knox, going to GreenBay and leaving Babylon but what was the most betraying to him was her not being able to love him the way he wanted her too. Nevertheless, she still tried to repair the damage their friendship suffered and she had made progress over the last couple of years, but she still missed the old days when they were happy.

Thinking of David, Gabriella's mind went to Knox. The decisions she made regarding him was anything but easy and there were days, small moments where she almost regretted the choice she made. The thought of Knox always stun a little every so often. Gabriella could never forget how much she had loved him, how much she still loved him spite everything. Leaving Knox was the hardest thing she had ever done; but she knew that no matter how much they might have loved each other, how much he loved her; he would always be thinking of her mother

Alice; deep in the back of his mind; even if he didn't realize it himself. Gabriella could feel the difference of a man thinking solely of her and of him imagining her as someone she could never be. Gabriella could never regret her time with Knox, he was her first everything and she could she would never stop loving him. He who had taught her how and what it meant too truly love a person.

Of course, every time something happened in Gabriella's life or anytime she felt the need to talk about the choices she made, Gabriella would still see Dr. Wiseman. He had agreed to continue to see her as his patient via email and phone and of course, anytime she came home to Babylon. Dr. Wiseman had also given Gabriella the name of a college who was in GreenBay so she would have someone nearby.

As Gabriella daydreamed of the past and doodled on her essay, her mind wandered to all the things she had in her life know. Faith Mills her roommate and best friend. Gabriella still wasn't sure how they became friends, it all just happened. Faith literally ran into Gabriella one day scattering everything they were both carrying and as they were picking everything up Faith decided it was fate and that they were meant to be the very best of friends. She was right and Gabriella was glad to have a friend.

Gabriella managed to get her mind back on her essay to the point where she didn't notice the tall man standing in her bedroom doorway. He was very quiet as he stood watching Gabriella at her desk swaying back and forth softly in her small black chair, writing away, taking pauses as her mind wandered off; he always loved watching her write; he felt she was always so animated while writing no matter the subject. Every move and jester she made while writing seemed beautiful to him.

The man slowly and quietly walked through the door threshold and came up behind Gabriella's chair and gently wrapping his arms around her, leaning in taking in her sent; he lightly kissed the base of her neck. Gabriella didn't panic, she recognized the touch, the feel of his lips on her skin; the man's sent. She leaned back into him closing her eyes as he tightened his grip on her hugging her as he kissed her again. After a moment of embracing each other, the man moved his lips to her ear. He had something important to tell her and he wanted to insure he used the right words. He searched for Gabriella's favorite quote in his mind.

Gabriella loved to read, what she would do is pick a book, read it then go and watch the film of it. Throughout all the books and films, she had been through; Gabriella found that two held her favorite moments. Like most women, Gabriella fell victim to loving Jane Austen's novels and like most women; she had fallen for Mr. Darcy. Gabriella loved the moment where Darcy is first telling Elizabeth that he's in love with her and asks for her hand. What Gabriella loved most was Elizabeth's courage to turn him down. Gabriella's other favorite quote comes from a film she saw called Austenland. There is a moment in the film where the two main characters Jane Hayes and Henry Nobley are speaking about fantasies and how Nobley was wondering if he was her fantasy. Later in the film when Nobley is declaring himself to Jane, he brings back their conversation about fantasies and Gabriella simply fell in love with two of his quotes, Nobley said:

"Is it possible that someone like me could make you happy? Would you let me try?" and *"Have you ever stopped to consider that you may have this all backwards? Jane – you are my fantasy."*

Gabriella's lover knew all of this of course so when he went to find the words to express himself to her, he pulled from these stories. So gently whispering into Gabriella's ear, he found his words:

"You must allow me to tell you how ardently I admire and love you. Gabriella you are my fantasy; is it possible for a man like me to make you happy? Will you let me try?" And with his final question he pulled a small black box from his jacket pocket and placed it open before her.

Gabriella finally opened her eyes to find a vintage diamond ring before her waiting to be slipped on her finger. She put the ring on her left finger as she spun her chair around finally facing her lover brushing her hand against his cheek feeling the stubble already growing back from his morning shave; admiring his gentle smile and bright blue eyes as she leaned in giving him a proper kiss.

"Yes" Gabriella said, between each kiss she gave him. She was happy, she had found herself her very own Austen hero and she was never letting him go.

Their celebration kiss turned and grew passionate and all consuming. Gabriella's lover intended to make passionate love to her and she wasn't about to stop him. He lifted Gabriella from her chair up onto her desk pushing the chair out of the way with his foot and moved closer to Gabriella leaving no space between them. He could feel her heartbeat with anticipation as she wrapped her legs around his torso pulling him even closer into her as her fingers found each button of his blue-collared shirt. As his shirt fell to the floor, he lifted her white tank top off her letting it fall besides his. As he kissed her favorite part of her neck he scooped her up in his arms and turned over to the bed, shedding the rest of their clothes and allowing their desire for each other take control. They had made love before many times but this time was different, this time was with a promise of forever.

The two of them laid in Gabriella's now messy bed tangled in each other having one of those post lovemaking moments where their facing each other with their arms wrapped around the other staring into each other's eyes. Gabriella loved his bright blue eyes; she could always loose herself in them, as she was staring out into the vast open ocean; that was one of the first things she had noticed about him. Well after his soft English accent of course. Gabriella laid next to her wonderful man feeling like the luckiest woman in the world, wondering how she became so happy after so many years of pain and misery. Gabriella started to run her fingers through his fine slightly wavy dirty blond hair as she leaned in for another kiss when she saw the time on her clock sitting on her bedside table. Gabriella took her kiss, which he willing gave then motioned for the need of getting out of bed.

"So, I have to kick you out love so I can get back to work and try to finish my essay." Gabriella gave a slight smirk indicating that she didn't truly want him to leave. "And I also have to get ready to meet Faith for dinner."

"I know." He said with his dreamy accent that always made Gabriella melt. "Faith and I planned the dinner to celebrate our engagement. Oh and there will be others there too so try to act surprised please." He gave her his most adorable smirk knowing that it always made her smile and giggle slightly and this time was no expectation. Gabriella stole another kiss.

Gabriella's fiancé left letting himself out while Gabriella laid in bed a few moments longer dreaming of her sexy Englishman. Coming back down to earth and knowing all the things, she had to do, Gabriella put her cloths back on, placing her chair back in its place and tried to get back to work. As Gabriella tried to focus, she kept thinking about all the people she wanted to tell about her upcoming wedding and she knew the exact person to tell first. Gabriella grabbed her cell and dialed Dr. Wiseman. Their conversation didn't last long, she just told him the happy news how she was planning for them to come out and visit once she graduated. Dr. Wiseman congratulated her and told her he was looking forward to their visit, after her phone call to Dr. Wiseman Gabriella wrote a letter to Mr. Knox. Through her four years at GreenBay College Gabriella and Knox kept in contact through letters, like they use to do back in high school. Gabriella had been putting off the news of her lover to Knox not because she didn't want him to know but because she wasn't sure she was ready for him to know that she didn't wait for him; that she had moved on.

Sealing Knox's letter and putting it aside Gabriella got back to her English Lit essay. She had just shy of an hour and a half to finish her essay and get ready for dinner when she heard knocking on her front door.

'Knock, knock. Knock, knock'

She wanted to ignore the knocking, as she really needed to finish her paper. Gabriella was in her final two months of GreenBay College and was about to graduate with a degree in History of English Literature.

'Knock, knock. Knock, knock'.

Gabriella dropped her head down on her desk. Frustrated, she started to mutter to herself.

"Alright, alright. Not like I'm trying to work or anything." Gabriella stood up from her desk and headed towards the door where the persistent tapping was coming from.

Gabriella Harris was 23 years old, 5ft tall and slightly larger than she should be, but still healthy. She was dressed in a white tank top and light faded blue jeans with black sneakers. She was simple and average looking, not the most beautiful woman in the world, though not without beauty either.

Gabriella's hair was slightly curly and auburn in colour. It reached just below her shoulders; her hair colour almost matched her wide hazel eyes that had seen a lifetime of pain in just a few short years.

She had scars on her face, just below her cheek which continued all the way down to her neck; still noticeable, but they had faded greatly over the years. Gabriella had gotten so used to her scars, but she would never forget how she received them. Her father had taken his half-empty beer bottle to her when she was around 14; he had done this out of rage and drunkenness. To him, Gabriella looked too much like her mother, his late wife, and he could not bear to look at her. After that, he was deemed mentally insane, and was sent to the Ridgefield Mental Institution.

The person banging on Gabriella's front door was quite persistent and as Gabriella moved towards the door, she thought that perhaps it could be her roommate, Faith.

Faith was always forgetting or losing her keys and Gabriella imagined that Faith had most likely locked herself out thinking only of the engagement dinner and had come home a bit early from class to get ready. The two girls lived together in their small two-bedroom apartment, which was only five minutes away from the College.

'*Knock, knock.*'

"Alright! Calm down, I'm coming; I'm coming; just hold on a minute!" Gabriella reached the front door and opened it, prepared to be annoyed, only to be surprised by who was on the other side of it.

"Oh, Hi; I haven't seen you in well… ages. What, uh, what brings you all the way out here?" Her unexpected visitor caught her off guard but she greeted her guest cheerfully nonetheless. "Hey… hey wait! No hey! Wait, what… what are you doing? HEY, NO, *STOP!* STOP!"

Chapter Fifteen: Panic

"What have you done? What have you done? Oh God, God what have you done?" He sat on the floor, back against the door leading down into the basement. He rocked back and forth against the door and he couldn't stop shaking. Rocking, staring down at his hands that were dripping with blood. "How did this happen? How'd it come to this? Oh God, oh God, what have you done?"

The young man continued to mutter to himself as he tried to drown out the screaming coming from his basement. He kept his eyes shut tight, hoping that that would maybe make this all just a bad dream. He knew better though, this was no dream. He rocked his body harder against the door, while his muttering grew louder.

"What have you done? God what have you done?" Asking himself repeatedly, hoping the answer might magically appear to him.

After a while, he noticed that the screaming had stopped and that he had finally calmed down a bit. The rocking had stopped and he decided that it was time to go wash the blood off his hands. He got up and moved towards the kitchen, where the sink was. It was then that he heard singing. She was singing.

"Amazing Grace, how sweet the sound
That saved a wretch like me!"

He couldn't believe what he was hearing.

"I once was lost, but now I am found
Was blind but now I see!"

This was her prayer, her salvation: God, her Faith. She put all her trust and her life in the belief that God would save her.

"At least she's not screaming anymore." He said to himself as he washed his hands over the sink. 'Now what?' questions were still forming in his head. Unsure of what to do next, he stood at the sink with the hot water running uselessly over his hands. He watched as the water, which was pink with blood turn clear. He was lost in thought trying to determine what to do next.

By the time, he realized his hands were clean; they had turned red yet again, this time from the hot water. He turned off the water and grabbed the towel on the side of the counter, drying his hands as he did so. After that, he headed towards the basement door.

"How precious did that grace appear?
The hour I first believed"

His prisoner was still singing, sobbing and crying as she pushed out each and every verse of 'Amazing Grace'. He could hear her tears in every word she sang. He stood in front of the door, leaning his head gently against it as he listened to her sing. He found that as she sang tears began to form and fall from his own dark eyes. Her voice, sweet as it was, was shaky, full of fear and terror. She sang to bring comfort to herself in hopes of calming down from the painful events of the day.

He kept wiping his eyes, the tears not stopping, no matter how hard he willed them too. Her voice was so soft and soothing, despite being riddled with fear. In a different setting he would have thoroughly enjoyed her voice; but not today, not like this. Knowing that today she sang from pain and suffering gave him little enjoyment.

As he listened to her, he started to mutter to himself again. "What have you done? How, how could you do this to her? You know what she's been through, how much she's already suffered and endured. How could you do this? How the hell did it even come to this? What the hell are you going to do now? How do you plan to get out of this one? Better question: what are you supposed to do with him? Never mind her, what about him?"

His last thought toyed with him for a moment. He knew he would have to go down into the basement and at least deal with him. He hadn't planned for any of this, taking them that is. All of it was spur of the moment. He had been completely out of his mind, consumed with rage. Now he had no idea what to do, where to go from here. He was still trying to comprehend what had happened, still trying to wrap his head around his actions.

He tried to gather himself together, placing his hand on the door-knob, preparing to go down and deal with the mess he had created. As he took a deep breath to steady himself, he could still hear her singing.

"When we've been there,
Ten thousand years
Bright shining as the sun"

He exhaled slowly and turned the doorknob, opening the basement door. He could hear her so much clearer with the door open. He took one more deep breath than headed down the squeaky staircase, leaving the basement door open for light. With each and every step he took his prisoner's voice grew louder and louder. He managed to make his way down to the last step of the staircase but that's as far as he got.

The basement was large, dark, and dreary. There were four large beams made of cement supporting the ceiling. The only other light apart from the open basement door came from two small windows and a lamp placed on the far right side. There wasn't a lot of stuff down there; some boxes with unknown contents, an old worn out stand up kicking bag, an old freezer big enough to hold a body in, and an old hospital bed with Gabriella Harris handcuffed to it.

The sight of her had him frozen to his spot on the bottom step. He had handcuffed her to the metal headboard, and she was sitting on the top of the bed, gently pulling at the cuffs as she sang. He could see blood trickling down her wrists around the cuffs; her face was bruised and cut; blood running down the right side of her from where he had hit her in the course of taking her. Gabriella's white tank top was stained with dirt and blood; her jeans were torn at the left knee and had just as many stains as her shirt. Her eyes were shut tight, as if she did not wish to see her surroundings as she sang, maybe pretending to be in a different place, a less scary place.

> *"We've no less days, to sing God's praise*
> *Then when we first begun"*

He watched her, listened to her scared, shaky voice push out each word.

> *"Amazing grace, how sweet the sound*
> *That saved a wretch like me,*
> *I once was lost but now I am found*
> *Was blind but now I see"*

"I always did love to hear you sing." As she fell silent, he couldn't help himself from speaking. Gabriella opened her puffy hazel eyes and looked up to face her abductor. She couldn't see his face due to the lack of light in the room, but she certainly recognized his voice. Gabriella was slightly disoriented from her head wound, but the sound of his voice made her angry and fearful and put her full alert. It took her a few seconds before she spoke to her kidnapper.

"Why... why are you doing this? Please, I-I don't understand. Why?" Tears started to fall from her puffy eyes, down her cheeks.

He stood firm in his place, arms crossed hard against his chest. He shook his head back and forth, dropping it slightly. "You never did get it, did you?" He wasn't sure why he responded the way he did. He hardly understood what he was doing himself. It had all happened so fast. But he made his voice sound strong and firm, full of anger, making the statement believable even to himself.

As Gabriella was trying to understand what was going on. Kenneth Madson started to come to. He was the poetry professor at GreenBay College. He was Gabriella's teacher. Kenneth Madson was a tall lean man with sandy blond hair, dark blue eyes, and a goatee. He was in his mid-40s and was never seen in anything but a suit, he believed that by looking professional, one was professional.

Everything for Kenneth was a bit blurry, but soon his eyes started to adjust and things started to focus. "Umm... what's, ah, what's going on?" Kenneth asked; a little confused. He struggled to shift his current position of sitting on the cold, hard concrete floor. As he looked around the dark basement his eyes focused in on Gabriella and his heart began to race with fear for her, fear for them both.

"Gabs, Gabriella... are you okay? Are you hurt?" His voice was brimming with terror. Gabriella shifted her glared from their abductor over to Kenneth, her gaze softening on the latter person.

"Yes, I'm alright. Are you?"

"I... um. I think so?" He was trying to hide the fear in his voice as he replied to Gabriella.

Their abductor watched the two them exchange looks of worry. He started to grow very tired and impatient with their concern for each other and cleared his throat to gain their full attention. Gabriella and Kenneth turned their heads back over to the man and waited for him to speak.

"Right," he began, "So how long have you two been an item then?"

Both Gabriella and Kenneth shared a confused look. 'He's insane' they thought, and turned back to their abductor, giving him the same confused look. Neither of them had any idea what he was talking about. Gabriella went to speak, but Kenneth spoke before she could even utter a single word.

"Item? What do you mean 'item'? Item as in together? You think the two of us are... what, a couple?" Kenneth paused, waiting for a reply to any of his questions.

"Yes." Their abductor said after a moment, trying to figure out where he was going with all of this. "Yes I believe you to be a couple... so, how long?" Kenneth couldn't believe they were having this conversation. "We're not... we're friends, that's all. Just friends."

Gabriella was looking back and forth between Kenneth and their abductor while the two men glared at each other. She wanted to jump in and say something, but she hardly knew what to say.

"Really? I know her," the abductor said, pointing over to Gabriella, "So please, don't insult me by saying that there's nothing between the two of you; or don't you know professor? Teachers are just her type." He shifted his gaze over to Gabriella as he said his next piece. "She likes older, unavailable, literary men. They'd likely have a Scottish accent; but hey, I guess he was just a one off. You know it's funny Gabriella I could have sworn that you believed him to be the absolute love of your life; but maybe I was mistaken, especially if you've got this one wrapped around your finger." All the tears from earlier were gone from his dark eyes, and now he knew why he had taken her, jealousy. There was nothing left in him but jealousy, anger, and betrayal.

Gabriella could hardly believe what she was hearing. Her tone was indignant as she spoke, "That's... that's what this is all about? Seriously? You've got to be joking... you honestly think...?" Gabriella's anger got the best of her causing her to silence herself.

Poor Kenneth was completely out of the loop in all of this and he was simply trying to keep up with everything. There was clearly a thing he was unaware of, and the two of them probably had a deep long history.

"Well we all have our types don't we?" the abductor said in a very snide tone.

"Oh, well yeah, and we all know your type, don't we?" Gabriella was being as cheeky as she could, knowing he wouldn't actually do anything about it.

"Don't give me that, you know full well my type. It just happens to be the same as a certain English teacher we both know." He had finally moved off the bottom step of the staircase and was standing right in front of Gabriella, trying desperately to contain his temper. Gabriella was too angry to be afraid of him at this point, so did very little to control her own anger.

"You cannot be serious, we've been over this I don't know how many times... so I'm sorry but... but just get over it okay? You can't force me to have feeling for you! So would you please, for the love of God, move on already. Get over it." Gabriella was sitting as far forward on the bed as she could, the cuffs pulling against her wrists but she hardly felt the pain; her body and mind had been consumed by fury.

Their abductor backed away from Gabriella and moved towards Kenneth, who still had no idea what was going on. The abductor's anger and rage was in full control at this point; and knowing he wouldn't be able to take it out on Gabriella. He stood over Kenneth and kept his dark eyes on Gabriella. He looked as though he had more to say but instead of speaking, he started to kick Kenneth in the ribs causing him to yell out in pain falling to his side curling his legs up to his chest. As he kept kicking Kenneth on the ground, he started to yell over at Gabriella.

"How long have you been with this one then? The full four years or is he simply this year's teacher? Or even this month's?" His jealousy consumed him completely as he continued to kick Kenneth; he watched the fear in Gabriella's eyes rise again.

Gabriella screamed back to him, begging him to stop but that only seemed to fire him up more, causing him to beat harder and harder on Kenneth. He finally looked down at Kenneth and stopped kicking him for a moment to ask a question.

"You like screwing your students then? Is that the type of teacher you are?" He didn't allow Kenneth to reply. Kenneth was still doubled over in pain, hands still cuffed behind his back. Their abductor looked back over at Gabriella, then back down at Kenneth, and started to beat him again.

Gabriella screamed and screamed at him to stop but there was nothing she could do. She pulled at the cuffs deepening her cuts, trying to free herself but she was not strong enough. She yelled and pleaded to no end. Their abductor wasn't listening to Gabriella anymore, to her screams; his rage and anger consumed his body rendering him incapable to stop himself, and to do anything but beat upon Kenneth.

Kenneth's cuffs had broken away during the beating and he had fallen completely onto his side on the cold cement floor. He was far too weak to defend himself. With every blow to Kenneth, Gabriella screamed and yelled louder and louder, with tears rolling down her bruised face.

"Stop it! Please, you're *killing* him. Please stop, *please stop*. You're killing him! Stop!"

Chapter Sixteen: Trust

"John? John, have you heard from Gabriella lately?"

John Montgomery sat in his chair at the kitchen table, trying to ignore his wife as he read the evening paper. John Montgomery was a simple man, tall and lanky, and always looked very tired. He was well into his late fifties, retired from the navy. John liked the simple things. The navy had made him a man of routine, which he really didn't mind but he was not good with change.

When his niece Gabriella Harris came to live with him and his wife Enid, he struggled with the upheaval at first, but over time, he grew quite fond of her.

John could still hear his wife Enid asking him questions about their niece so he lowered his paper just enough to look over at his wife and said, "No, I haven't." Then raised the paper back up and continued reading. Enid gave John an unimpressed look then continued talking.

"Well, I'm worried; it's been a month since we've heard from her; no letter, not even a phone call! Nothing! It's not like her." Enid Montgomery was talking fast, unable to control her speed of speech. Worry and fear was apparent her tone as she spoke to her husband.

Enid Montgomery was in her late forties, frail and very petite. She was the sister of Gabriella's father. Enid was the complete opposite of her husband, John. He liked the quiet life; Enid liked the rush of society. She had to be in everyone's business, no matter what.

Enid stopped talking again, staring over at her husband, annoyed that he wasn't more concerned for their niece. John could feel his wife's eyes on him, so again he lowered the paper and looked up at her.

"She's probably just busy. Aren't her final exams coming up soon? She's most likely studying for them. I'm sure when she's done she'll call. Besides, we're going up in two months for the graduation ceremony, we'll see her then." John's attempt to console his wife was futile at best. Once she set her mind on something there was no changing it. Enid started shaking her head in disbelief.

"No, no, even during exam time she always called; let us know how she was doing. Something is wrong John, I'm telling you! I know something is... I can feel it." Enid took a breath and John went to speak, but Enid started talking again, not giving him a chance to get a word in.

"Maybe I should call the college? Do you think? See if she's going to her classes, find out how's she's doing? Or maybe call her roommate, Faith and..." John cut her off there completely, shaking his head.

"No, no, she's fine! Do nothing. Please let it be. I have no doubt we will hear from Gabriella in a day or two. Just let it be, my dear." John then stood from the table, grabbed his paper, and walked out of the kitchen away from his bantering wife.

A few days went by and Enid was still worried about her niece, Gabriella. They still hadn't heard from her and Enid's paranoia was only growing. Enid knew that John wasn't worried and was not interested in repeating the conversation they had had a few days ago, though Enid refused to drop it. That evening, when they sat down for dinner, Enid decided to bring it up again. Just as Enid went to speak, the phone started to ring and she rushed over to answer it in the hopes of it being Gabriella.

As Enid answered the phone, John watched with the same hope Enid had. Even though John did not show his concern for Gabriella, he certainly did feel it.

"Hello? Gabs?" Enid's voice was fast and heavy; she was trying to control her breathing as she spoke.

"Ah... no sorry Mrs. Montgomery; It's Faith, Gab's roommate." There was a slight pause over the line from both sides, until Enid could compose herself enough to speak.

"Oh Faith dear, how are you?"

"Umm well, I'm a bit troubled at the moment. Ah, is Gabs there by chance?"

"No." Enid's voice raised an octave as she spoke, causing John to stand from his chair. "Ah, she hasn't been home since Christmas." Enid continued, "She should be there with you, finishing school."

John was standing by his wife now, trying to listen in as Faith spoke.

"Well, I haven't, umm... actually seen or heard from Gab's in about two weeks now. That's why I called. At first I thought that Gab's might have just needed a bit of time and space with all the change happening. I figured she'd be back in a day or two especially with finals just around the corner but she never did. Then I thought perhaps she went home and didn't call but..." Faith cut herself off, too upset to continue.

Enid was shaking her head, trying to take in what Faith was saying. John grabbed the phone out of Enid's hand and had her go sit down to gather herself while he finished talking to Faith.

"Faith, its John here; what exactly are you telling us here?" John's voice was calm and stable. He knew he needed to be the calm one.

"I, I don't know where Gabs is. I've asked around, teachers, other students, no one has seen her. I filed a missing person's report with both campus security and the local police, but they're both saying the same thing! They told me she's probably just gone off somewhere! They figured Gabs dropped out and went home. That's why I decided to call. I'm worried about her Mr. Montgomery; I don't believe she dropped out. I think maybe... maybe someone has her." Faith fell silent again, allowing John to process what he was hearing.

"What makes you think someone has her Faith?" John asked after a second or two, trying to understand everything.

"Well because... and at first I didn't think anything of it but... that first day Gabs was gone I came home to our front door being slightly open and a chair had been knocked over. I told the police, but they said she was most likely in a rush. But I don't believe that."

"Alright" John started, "Alright Faith it's going to be alright. Thank you for calling and I will see what I can find out. I promise to call if I get some news okay?"

"Okay. Thanks Mr. Montgomery." Faith hung up.

John put the phone down and looked at his wife. She was still shaking her head, back and forth in disbelief. John stood there, watching Enid, trying to decide what to do. He looked over to the clock on the kitchen stove, 10 after 6; too late to call the college but not the police down there. He looked back at Enid to find her unchanged, then picked up the phone and dialed the police.

Half an hour later John had the same story the police at given Faith. He was thoroughly unimpressed. John could feel his temper grow from being given the run-around by the people who were meant to protect. Phone in hand he took a seat at the kitchen table across from Enid and tried to think of anyone who would help or know where Gabriella might be.

His mind automatically gave him two names; one he was fine with, the other he was not. John looked down at the phone he was holding then back to his wife. "Enid dear," his voice was soft and quiet as he spoke to her, "Enid, I think you should go lie down, get some rest. I'll sort things out, okay?"

Enid didn't say anything; she didn't even look up at John. She nodded her head, stood up from her chair and headed upstairs to bed. John waited to hear the bedroom door close before dialing the phone. He was calling David Thompson.

David Thompson had been Gabriella's best friend for years. They became friends shortly after John and Enid had taken Gabriella in. David was the same age and just as bright as Gabriella was; he was slightly less ambitious in what he wanted in life. John had always liked David and noticed what a loyal friend he was.

John let the phone ring a good half a dozen times before giving up. David had no answering machine so there was no way for John to leave a message. He hung up feeling very discouraged; he hoped David could help him, not wanting to call his other option. John set the phone down on the table then moved over to the fridge and grabbed a beer. He decided he needed a drink before making his next phone call. He sat back down, beer in hand looking at the table. Dinner was fully laid out going cold from the events of the evening. John took a large gulp from his beer, almost consuming it in one swallow. He set the beer down, grabbed the phone and dialed.

He was calling Aidan Knox. Knox had been Gabriella's English Teacher through High School, but he also been her lover. John disliked Knox for that reason; he believed that Knox had deceived Gabriella into loving him so he could live out his fantasies he had about Gabriella's mother Alice. Knox had known and loved Alice when they were in school.

The phone rang only a couple of times before Knox answered. "Hello." Knox's Scottish accent seemed thicker than John remembered.

"Hi, is this Aidan Knox? The English teacher at Babylon High?" John was double-checking he had the right man.

"Yes, may I ask whose calling?"

"John Montgomery, Gabriella Harris' uncle." There was silence over the line; John could hear Knox breathing slowly.

"What can I do for you Mr. Montgomery?" Even through Knox's accent, John could hear the surprise in his voice.

"Is Gabriella with you?" John chose to skip the formality of small talk and get right to his point.

"Ah... no sorry, she's not." Knox tried to keep the curiosity out of his voice as he answered, but it slipped out anyways, "What makes you ask?"

"Because no one's seen her in a couple of weeks and I know the two of you had an affair. I thought the two of you might have started up again." John was uncommonly blunt regarding the topic; he did not wish to be misunderstood "And," John continued, "If by any chance she wasn't with you I thought you might know where she is. I know you two still talk at least." John stopped there to give Knox a chance to respond.

"What do you mean no one's seen her for two weeks?" Knox was trying to get a grasp on what he was being told so John filled him in on what he knew.

Filling Knox in on the situation did nothing to help John find Gabriella. He had asked Knox to keep an eye out or let him know if he heard anything from anyone. Knox agreed to help in any way he could in which John was grateful for even though he did not show it. The conversation did not go any farther than that. Both men knew better than to ask any personal details.

John hung up the phone after talking to Knox and headed upstairs to check on Enid. His conversation with Knox did not ease any part of his mind regarding his niece. John walked into their bedroom and saw Enid lying in bed, quietly crying. John lay down next to her, and took her in his arms and started to cradle her. "It's going to be alright, I promise, we'll find her." John did his best to sooth his wife until she fell asleep.

The next morning John decided to file his own missing person's report to his local police station. He told them everything he had learned which wasn't much. He asked them to get in touch with the station in GreenBay to see if they could find out anything more. John left the police all of his contact information. They took down everything but told him the same thing the GreenBay station had told him. They tried to make John understand that Gabriella might have simply run away. Their disinterest with the situation made John's blood boil and could tell the police were not going to be any help.

John spent over an hour at the station answering questions about Gabriella: what she was like, who her friends were, who her family was, and who she might be seeing; if anyone. The only possibility that the police could come up with was that her father broken out of the mental facility and taken Gabriella. They told John they would look into it.

When John was done talking to the police, he just sat in his car feeling very discouraged. He wasn't sure what else he could do. John thought maybe he could drive up to GreenBay and check things out for himself but he knew he couldn't leave Enid for too long, and going up there would mean a few days away.

Enid was refusing to get out of bed. He was worried about what all of this was doing to his wife and did not want her to be alone. After a few moments of really thinking things through, he knew what he needed to do. He turned his car on and drove over to Babylon High.

Chapter Seventeen: Request

John sat in the high school parking lot for almost 10 minutes convincing himself that this was the best thing to do. He had to think of Gabriella and put his personal feelings aside. As John walked into the high school classroom, he saw the man who had given his niece so much heartache. John saw this forty-one year old man with a bit more grey hair than the last time John had seen him. Nevertheless, it was the same 6", lean, unshaved stubble looking Scotsman sitting at his desk grading papers. Knox looked up from his desk when John entered.

"Mr. Montgomery... what are you doing here?" Aidan Knox stood quickly from his desk and reached out his hand to greet John; surprised to see him in his classroom. John stopped just in front of the desk and shook Knox's hand.

"Mr. Knox I'm sorry to come but, but I need your help." It pained John to ask but he saw no other way. He could not personally go out and find Gabriella; he thought that maybe Knox could. Knox invited John to sit down.

"Please Mr. Montgomery how can I help you?" Knox understood that this was hard for John to come to him and he was happy to try to help find Gabriella if he could.

The two men sat in silence for a moment, avoiding direct eye contact. John let his eyes wander across Knox's desk; looking over the piles of papers and books. He had student's assignments in the center with a red pen just off the side. He had been grading when John walked in. John also noticed a small picture frame and without even thinking, he picked it up to take a closer look.

The photo in the frame was of Knox and Gabriella. They were sitting under a large willow tree, a blanket under them; Knox was up against the tree while Gabriella was leaning into him with his arms wrapped around her. Knox's eyes were closed while Gabriella was looking down into a book. Knox had his head tilted down pressing his cheek against hers. They were both smiling: happy and in love.

What John recognized in the photo was Gabriella's dress; it was the white sundress; he had bought her just before her final year of high school. He couldn't help but notice how happy Gabriella looked; He was trying to remember the last time he had actually even seen her that happy. He couldn't. John could feel Knox watching him examine the picture so he quickly put the photo back and gave Knox his attention.

"It's my favourite." Knox said as John put the picture back down. "We took that just before she left for GreenBay."

"Right" John wasn't quite sure how to respond. "You know... if I had known then, I would've stopped it. She didn't tell me until after."

"Well you would have tried."

"Yes, knowing Gabs she would have found a way." Both men had a small smile, thinking about Gabriella. Knox decided they were getting too off topic and thought he'd get things back on track.

"So, Mr. Montgomery, how can I help you?"

"Mr. Knox," John started, "I would like your help finding Gabriella. I know I have no right to ask but I really don't know what else to do. I've spoken to the police and campus security; I cannot get a hold of David, and I really have nowhere else to go. I know you care for her so I am asking... please." John went silent to give Knox a chance to respond.

"What did you have in mind?" Knox asked.

"Well if you could possibly go to GreenBay, talk to people up there. I would go however; I really cannot leave my wife Enid right now. She uh, didn't take the news well and she needs me right now but I need to find Gabriella so..." John went silent again; asking for help was not something he was very good at; he had always been a do it yourself kind of man.

"Well... I do have some time off that I can take so... so yeah I... I have no problem doing that, see what I can find out." Knox gave him a slight 'try not to worry' look and John actually seemed a bit relieved. He still wasn't Knox's biggest fan but he was grateful for the help.

"Thank you." John said as he stood up to leave stretching his hand out this time.

"Sure, no problem; just take care of your wife and I'll try to find Gabs." Knox stood as well taking John's hand to shake, the two men dropped hands again and John left to care for Enid, his mind slightly more at ease knowing Knox was going to help. John left leaving Knox to think about what he was about to do, trying to figure out a way to start finding Gabriella.

Knox sat back down in his chair and looked at his clock: 20 minutes left in his lunch hour, enough time to call David. He picked up the phone and dialed out the local mechanic shop where David worked. He thought he'd try to get David at work, and then at home if needed.

"Babylon Mechanics, how may we help you?" The receptionist was a peppy young girl who chewed bubble gum loud enough to hear on the other end of the line.

"Yes I'm looking for David Thompson is he in?" Knox was hopeful to find David at work.

"No sorry, he's on holiday; can I get you somebody else?"

"Ah, no... holiday for, for how long?"

"Don't know, a few weeks I think?"

"Okay, do you know if he left town or not?"

"No, no clue."

"Alright well thanks a lot love; you have a good rest of the day." Knox hung up the phone and grabbed his phone book to look up David's home number. After finding it and calling, and receiving no answer, Knox was starting to feel very discouraged in his search.

At the end of the school day Knox went and got the time off that he needed to find Gabriella. He was given two weeks so he desperately hoped it would not take that long. Leaving the school instead of going home, Knox headed to David's to see if he was home and simply ignoring his phone.

'Knock, knock. Knock, knock.'

The door opened slightly and all Knox could see was David's short brown hair and his very dark brown eyes. Knox was glad David was home.

"Hello David." Knox smiled slightly in hopes it would help but he knew it would not. David had never liked Knox simply for the reason that Knox got the one person David had ever loved: Gabriella.

David opened the door the rest of the way and took a step forward. David had changed since high school. He had filled out; built muscle, no longer the scrawny boy Knox knew. His hands were stained with oil from working on cars all day. Knox believed that to be the reason for David's newfound muscles.

"What do you want?" David was short with Knox; he wanted him to go away and Knox could feel it in his tone and manner.

"I tried calling but there was no answer; I need to talk to you about Gabriella. Look, I don't know if you've heard but she's gone missing."

"And what you're trying to be all prince charming and try and save her, find her? Whatever; get a life old man." David went to close the door but Knox put his hand up to stop it.

"Look, I know you don't like me but come on, it's Gabriella we're talking about. Now please, I came here to ask you to help me find her. I know you care about her; you must be worried about her, just a bit? She is your friend after all." Knox hoped reason would convince David but he was to set in his ways. There was too much anger and resentment for David, even to want to help.

"Let me tell you something, because of you I lost the only person I've ever loved. You poisoned her mind and she left. Gabriella and I haven't been friends in a long time now, so no, I'm not worried about her. I don't care."

"David you must care a little, she's..." Knox got cut off by David.

"Look I haven't seen that heartless bitch in almost three years so when I say I don't care, I mean I don't care. So do me a favor and piss off." David slammed to door in Knox's face, completing his point.

Knox could hardly believe David acted so heartless. David used to be a nice young man and there was never anyone as loyal. Knox banged on David's front door another half dozen times hoping he would come back and change his mind. Knox walked away feeling sorry for David; not being able to let go of the past to save Gabriella's future.

Chapter Eighteen: Questions

Knox lay in his bed, wide-awake. He kept thinking about his argument with David, about why he was dead set on not helping to find Gabriella. Had David's love for Gabriella really turned to hatred?

Knox's thoughts kept him turning all night, not letting him get any sleep. He tried to put his thoughts of David aside in order to figure out what to do next, to figure out just what he could do to help. After all, he was only an English teacher.

Knox decided that in the morning he would call Gabriella's old therapist Dr. Wiseman and see if he had any information about her. He thought that if Gabriella was in some sort of trouble she might go to him for help.

It was about nine in the morning the next day when Knox dug out Dr. Wiseman's number and gave him a call.

"Hello." Dr. Wiseman picked up on the second ring.

"Hi, my name is Aidan Knox and I was hoping you'd have some time today to meet with me. It's a matter of urgency."

"May I ask what this is regarding?"

"Ah yes... it's regarding Gabriella Harris. She used to be a patient of yours I believe."

There was a short pause over the line while Dr. Wiseman took in what he was being told.

"Sorry did you say Aidan Knox? As in Mr. Knox the English teacher over at Babylon High?" Dr. Wiseman wanted to know he was speaking to whom he thought he was speaking too.

"Ah, yes... that would be me. So do you have a time for a meeting Dr. Wiseman?"

There was another short pause between the two men.

"I'm sorry Mr. Knox but I cannot discuss my patient with anyone so..."

Mr. Knox cut Dr. Wiseman off at this point.

"No please you miss understand my intent Doctor! Gabriella's gone missing and I'm merely looking for information to find her."

It took Dr. Wiseman a second to take in all that Knox was saying. "Will 11 work for you Mr. Knox?"

"11 works just fine."

With two hours before his meeting with Dr. Wiseman, Knox decided to call the GreenBay College security in hopes of gaining any more information on Gabriella's disappearance. After sitting on hold for close to a quarter of an hour they gave him the same line they had given John; that Gabriella had simply run off. By the time, Knox got off the phone he had about 20 minutes to get to Dr. Wiseman's office. He grabbed his keys and headed across town.

Dr. Wiseman held his practice out of his home. He lived in a small residential area just on the outskirts of town. Babylon was a small town so it only took Knox about 10 minutes to get there. Knox parked out on the street in front of Dr. Wiseman's house and went around to the side gate. Following the path up to the side door; leading into his waiting room. The waiting room was empty; Knox looked around the small room while he waited for Dr. Wiseman.

The walls were a faded beige colour with three photographs on one wall and a clock on the other. There were chairs lined up neatly against the two walls with side tables between the chairs holding outdated magazines. The room reminded Knox of a Doctor's office.

Knox was too anxious to sit. He stood facing the three photos' looking back and forth between them. He didn't spend much time looking at the first and third photo. The first was a photo of mountains and the third was of a stream rushing with water. Knox spent his time focusing on the second photo. The waterfall with a pool of deep blue water beneath it in the heart of the waterfall you could just barely see the face of a man. Knox continued to shift in his spot trying to see the hidden face better.

Dr. Wiseman opened his office door to greet Knox, finding him looking at the center photo.

"The first time I met Gabriella she was staring at that photo. It fascinated her." Dr. Wiseman had startled Knox slightly, but after a second, he got himself together.

"It would," Knox, replied, "She always did love things that had an air of mystery to them. She always tried to figure out and understand everything." Knox examined the photo for another second before following Dr. Wiseman into his office. Dr. Wiseman took his seat in a large beige cushy chair, while Knox sat across from him on his matching couch.

Knox took a moment to examine Dr. Wiseman's office: Tall bookshelves overflowing with literature and a nook for coffee and tea. Knox noticed a Celtic cross on the wall, which made him smile.

"Your office is just as Gabriella described it." Knox said as he brought his attention back to Dr. Wiseman.

"Yes, it would be, I don't change this room much. I like it as it is." Dr. Wiseman figured Gabriella would have told Knox about their sessions or at least that she was talking to someone.

Knox continued to speak. "Gabs never really told me what you two talked about but she did tell me about your office and yourself. She always spoke very highly of you. You changed her life."

"I think we both changed her life, wouldn't you agree?"

They both sat in silence for a short moment letting Dr. Wiseman's last statement fill the room.

"So how can I help you? On the phone you said Gabriella had gone missing, is that right?"

"Yes she's missing. Her uncle has asked me to try to find her. The police are saying she simply ran off and the campus security at GreenBay is agreeing with them so no one's looking for her."

"Right and Gabriella's not the kind to just up and take off."

"Yes, so I was hoping you might be able to help me; I'm going to go up to GreenBay to see her roommate, Faith. I was wondering if you knew anyone else I should talk too. Out of curiosity when was the last time you saw or heard from Gabs?" Knox stopped talking to let Dr. Wiseman answer him.

"Well Gabriella and I didn't have a set schedule. The occasional phone call when she was overwhelmed by something. But I think the last time I saw her would have been Christmas when she was out here visiting everyone... however I did speak to her about two weeks ago."

Knox sat a little straighter when Dr. Wiseman said two weeks. Two weeks seemed to be the last time anyone spoke to her. Dr. Wiseman sat quietly allowing Knox to process everything.

"Two weeks seems to be the last time anyone has seen or heard from Gabs. So what happened two weeks ago?" Knox wasn't so much as asking the question as thinking aloud. "What did you two talk about? Was it just a check in call or was something wrong?"

Dr. Wiseman had to think a minute before answering Knox's question trying to determine how much to tell him. Gabriella had called to tell Dr. Wiseman about her engagement but not knowing if Gabriella was ready to tell everyone he felt he should keep that information to himself.

"Just a check in, nothing serious." Knox could see that there was more to Dr. Wiseman's call with Gabs but decided not to press it; he knew Dr. Wiseman could only divulge so much without breaking patient confidentiality.

Dr. Wiseman used the silence filling his office as a chance to ask a question or two of his own. "May I ask... how did you find out how Gabriella went missing?"

"Oh, from John Montgomery, Gab's uncle. He had phoned me to see if Gabs was with me. Then later he came and asked me for help. It seems the police, and the GreenBay Security are calling her a run-away." Dr. Wiseman could see how hard it was for Knox to say his last few words.

Knox continued. "I tried to talk to David but he... I don't know; he didn't seem himself. I mean we argued. He never did approve of Gabs and me, but this is beyond that. When I asked him to help me find Gabs, he not only refused but he actually told me he didn't care about any of it. He's become so bitter and angry." Knox stopped talking to focus again. David was not his concern, Gabriella was. Finding her, making sure she was safe was all he could think about; he couldn't afford any distractions.

"That was quite the triangle the three of you got into, but in the end, Gabriella made her choice."

"Yeah, and she chose neither of us." Knox interrupted.

"You do understand that Gabriella did what was best for her; she didn't make her choice lightly, but it was hers to make."

Silence filled the room again. Knox was trying to find a retort for Dr. Wiseman, but could find none. He knew the Doctor was right. After another minute, Knox started to speak. "I'm going to GreenBay, I want to speak to Gabs' roommate and if possible some of her classmates; see what I can find out."

Dr. Wiseman nodded his head in approval while Knox continued.

"Look, I was wondering if... do you think that maybe, maybe the cops are right and—"

Dr. Wiseman cut Knox off; he could see where he was going.

"No, I do not believe that Gabriella simply 'took off', she would never do that, and especially to the people she loves. It's not in her to give up and leave. She's too much of a fighter. Do you mind me asking when the last time you saw Gabriella was?"

"Well I heard from her a couple of months ago when I received her letter but I haven't seen her since Christmas when she was down visiting."

"So you two are corresponding?"

"Her idea, before we were together we used to write letters to each other, and she thought, seeing as she was away at school, letters would be a good way to stay in touch." Knox smiled to himself as he thought about all the letters over the years.

"Here's what I'm having trouble understanding and perhaps you are too." Dr. Wiseman began, "Gabriella has been missing for two weeks now right? Then why has no one contacted the Montgomery's for a ransom or anything? Where's the evidence of a kidnapping? Where's someone's motive? If she's been taken then why aren't there any demands? In two weeks, nothing!"

Knox put a very firm look on his face to hide his pains. He knew what Dr. Wiseman was going to suggest and he couldn't stop him from saying the words he'd been dreading most.

"As sad as it is, have you thought of the possibility that Gabriella may be dead?" Dr. Wiseman struggled to say his last sentence the thought filled him with grief but he knew that Knox needed to hear it.

The two men allowed silence to fill the room again as Knox struggled with what he had heard. His fear of Gabriella's death was something he could not deal with and Dr. Wiseman could see that plain as day; Knox needed to believe Gabriella was still alive, still somewhere in this world, waiting. He needed to believe that she was in a place where he could still save her. Dr. Wiseman realized that Knox could live in the world without her by his side, knowing she was happy; what he could not endure was her being gone from this world. Knowing she was dead would be too much.

Dr. Wiseman watched as Knox tried to comprehend the thought consuming his mind. Dr. Wiseman gently cleared his throat after another minute to continue their conversation.

"I need to ask, why are you doing this? Why are you torturing yourself trying to find her?"

Knox looked up at Dr. Wiseman's eyes and said just four words, "Because, I love her."

Knox was resolved that nothing more could come by staying so he moved to leave but before he could fully stand Dr. Wiseman had one more thing to offer him. "Here's what I can do for you," as Dr. Wiseman said as Knox settled back into his seat, "Before Gabriella left for GreenBay I set her up with a friend of mine who lives there. His name is Trevor Beddingfeild; he's a fellow psychotherapist like myself, and he's very good. I'll also find out if he knows anything about Gabriella's disappearance and I'll also ask him to share everything he can with you." Dr. Wiseman went over to his desk and wrote out Dr. Beddingfeild's information for Knox. Knox stood from the couch and moved towards the door as Dr. Wiseman reached him, giving him the information.

"Thank you." Was all Knox was capable of saying. The men shook hands. They could gain no more information from each other. Dr. Wiseman assured Knox he would call Dr. Beddingfeild right away and then advised Knox to be careful.

"You have no idea where this path will lead you. Please watch your back. I hope you find her." Dr. Wiseman tried to hide the fear in his voice but failed. Knox nodded his head and left.

Chapter Nineteen: Inquiries

The next morning Knox was on the road by nine. It was the six-hour drive to GreenBay, but to Knox it felt more like twelve. His impatience and worry was causing him to experience time more slowly. When had finally made it to GreenBay Campus his hopes had risen. He decided to go in with the hope of finding answers and getting closer to finding Gabriella or at least to get a better idea of what had happened to her.

As Knox parked and got out of his car, he realized he had no idea where to go. It had been years since he had been to GreenBay. He wandered around a bit, seeing what had changed and what had stayed the same. He was amazed at how the campus looked the same but also different.

His college days with Alice flooded his mind as he walked around. He came across a bench he had Alice used to sit at, and he sat down and watched the scenery around him.

Buildings had been re-vamped, the campus was larger now, sections had been added and he noticed some things hadn't been touched at all.

The students were rushing around Knox as he sat. He took a breath and all his worry and fear for Gabriella got him standing again. He did not wish to waste any more time.

He took another deep breath and watched the busy campus. Alice kept flashing through his mind, the two of them together, having lunch under their favourite tree, their conversations about their classes, all the fun they had. His image of Alice morphed into Gabriella; Gabriella roaming around the campus as her mother had years before.

Knox stood from the bench and headed towards the office to see whom he could talk to about Gabriella.

The office was busy. Students and staff were all over the place, looking for papers, taking phone calls, people standing about engaged in conversations about classes or assignments. Knox stood in the help service line with a few people in front of him, waiting to ask their questions.

The line gradually trickled away, allowing Knox to move closer to the receptionist. Everything was in slow motion for Knox. Time was moving slowly he felt like he was going insane; Knox knew it was just his impatience, which made time seem more slow. Nevertheless, it irked him greatly; he just wanted Gabriella back home safe, but all he could see were all the people standing in front of him.

"Hey, how can I help you today sir?" The receptionist gave Knox a big smile as she greeted him; while he was just happy, it was his turn.

"Yes, Hi! I was wondering if you could give me any information on a student Gabriella Harris? She's gone missing."

"And you are... sir?"

"Aidan Knox! I am um... a family friend. Her uncle asked me to try to find her. So can you help me?"

The smile was gone from the receptionist's perky face. "Let me call the head of our campus security and see if he can help."

"Thank you." Knox's hope was gone again. He knew what they would say. Knox listened to the receptionist while she called the head of security.

"Hey Doug; I have a guy here asking about Gabriella Harris. Do you want to come and talk to him?" Knox stood anxiously as the perky receptionist was on the phone. Knox's patience was starting to where thin and he just wanted his questions answered. Then the receptionist spoke again. "Oh, okay. I'll send him over. Yeah... thanks Doug. Talk to you later." She hung up the phone and looked at Knox.

"Doug is our head of security so if you just go over to building eight and ask for him he'll be waiting for you. Have a nice day." She had her big smile back on her perky face. Knox gave her a small smile as he said his thanks and headed off to find building eight.

Knox wandered the campus looking for building eight, every time he'd come up to a building he'd try to find the number for the building but couldn't. Knox finally got fed up after walking around in circles and getting nowhere. He stopped a student walking by.

"Hi, excuse me, but could you tell me which building is eight?"

"Um... yeah! It's the third one on the right, just down there, dude." The student told him pointing in the direction for him and then walking off in the opposite direction.

It only took a couple of minutes to get to Building eight once Knox knew where he was. He walked right in and asked for Doug. Before the woman sitting at the front desk could answer, Doug spoke up from behind her, standing in his office doorway.

"I'm Doug, what can I do for you?"

"I'm wondering what you can tell me about a student who disappeared. Gabriella Harris?"

"Are you a cop?" Doug asked.

"No, I'm a family friend who's been asked to find her. Her family is very worried and no one seems to be doing anything to try and find her."

Doug stood silent for a moment, deciding whether to help Knox. After a moment, Doug told Knox to come into his office; Knox came through the door and Doug shut it behind him so his secretary couldn't hear their conversation. Doug took a seat at his desk while Knox sat across from him.

"So what can you tell me about Gabriella's disappearance?" Knox wasn't wasting anytime.

"Family friend? Tell me, if her family's worried, why aren't they here instead of you?" Doug wanted to make sure he was talking to someone who was actually connected to Gabriella and not someone who could be a part of her disappearance.

"Her Uncle John, John Montgomery; I believe you spoke to him shortly after learning about his niece's disappearance. Do you remember?" Doug nodded in agreement and allowed Knox to continue. "Well he wanted to come, but he needed to stay and look after his wife. She's not taking all this well, as you can imagine."

Doug kept silent but showed his agreement with Knox's words.

"So seeing as I've known Gabriella for several years, and I also knew her late mother before, John asked me to find her. So that's what I plan to do." Knox tried to hide his impatience, but he was frustrated, he knew Doug was just doing his job, but Knox's worry for Gabriella clouded everything.

Doug believed Knox, he remembered having his conversation with John Montgomery, and so he decided to be honest with Knox. "Honestly, I don't know what's happened to Gabs. I wish I did. I checked her apartment and nothing seemed out of place. If someone took her, they certainly cleaned up after themselves. The only thing that seemed a miss was an oil residue on the outside of the doorknob, and there was a print but not enough to get an identity off of it." Doug looked down at his desk, taking a small breath before continuing. "You know, I really liked Gabs. She was really nice and sweet and had a good caring heart. Not many people are like that anymore. I do really hope she's doing okay, wherever she is but I can only do so much. I've given everything I have to the police and it's out of my hands. I'm sorry that I can't help you. I've spoken to all of Gabs' friends and teachers except one. But no one's seen or heard from her."

Knox could see Doug's sincerity and knew that he'd done all he could for Gabriella. One thing did tweak his interest though.

"You said you spoke to Gabs' teachers except one. Why didn't you talk to that teacher?"

"I couldn't, he's missing too. He's the school's Renaissance poetry Professor. His name is Kenneth Madson, nice guy. He disappeared around the same time as Gabs did." Doug decided to give Knox a minute to process the new information.

"Um, do you know… is there any connection between Gabs and Kenneth Madson? Besides him being her teacher that is" Knox was trying to see if the two disappearances were related at all.

"Umm, yeah! After her first year in his class, they became friends. As far as I know, Gabs took most of Kenneth's classes. You'd normally find them together. Always talking about poetry those two or some kind of literature. But that's not so uncommon here. The staff and students all act like a big family. That's the benefit of being in a small college I guess."

Knox couldn't help but smile at Doug's news. Gabriella had loved anyone she could have a decent literary conversation with.

"Were they a couple? Do you know? I mean if they were always together..." Knox stopped talking. His question hadn't come out quite as he had hoped. Doug was a bit taken aback from the question. It wasn't what he was expecting.

"Ah, no; they weren't a couple. Gabs' is involved with someone; he has nothing to do with the college. Don't remember what he does though, something to do with people... helping people, something like that anyways. Well I think I've told you all that I can." Doug stood from his desk and held his hand out for Knox to take. Knox rose and shook hands with Doug, thanking him for everything, and then left to ponder everything he'd been told.

Chapter Twenty: Roommate

'Knock, knock.' Knox stood waiting at Gabriella and Faith's front door, hoping Faith was home.

'Knock, knock.' after the fourth knock, Faith unlocked the door. She cautiously opened the door just enough to see who was on the other side.

"Can I help you?" She had fear in her voice but tried to maintain it.

"Yes, I'm Aidan Knox, a friend of Gabriella's, are you Faith?" Faith opened the door the rest of the way. When she heard him say his name, most of her fear vanished and she knew he was safe.

"Yes, I'm Faith, please come in." Faith moved out of the doorway to let Knox in then quickly shut and locked the door again. Faith led Knox down their small hallway and into their living room and offered him a seat.

"She'd talked about you, you know. She said she'd never been with a better man then you." Faith was attempting small talk, while she moved to the kitchen to boil the kettle for tea.

"I'm sorry... I should have recognized you from the photo right way. I've just been a bit off since Gabs went missing. I guess I'm afraid that someone's going to come back for me or something..." Faith trailed off when she started to fill the kettle and place it on the stove.

"Sorry," Knox was confused, "My picture?"

"Oh Yeah, Gabs keeps a picture of the two of you on her desk, next to the one of her and Trevor." Faith left the kitchen and headed to Gabs' room to grab the photos while Knox sat in confusion mouthing the name Trevor and wondering who he was. Moments later Faith came back holding two photo frames and handed them to Knox. The top one was of them together.

Knox smiled it was the same photo that he kept of them on his desk. Knox looked at the photo and remembered that day. He was happy then, being with her. Holding her safely in his arms, hopelessly believing she'd be there forever. Now when he sees the picture all he sees is what he no longer has. Knox set the photo on the coffee table, looked at the second one, and saw the happy couple. They were sitting in a bar booth, Gabriella was wrapped in the arms of a handsome, late thirties young man who Knox took to be Trevor.

Trevor's eyes were bright blue he had a wide smile and short wavy dirty blond hair. Trevor looked just as happy as Gabriella in the picture. The two of them were laughing at something, just enjoying life. It made Knox jealous. Knox regained his focus, putting the photo of Trevor and Gabriella next to the other one.

"They look like a happy couple. How long have they been together?" Knox's curiosity got the better of him; he wanted to know how serious they were. If Gabriella was as happy with him as they appear to be in the photo.

It took Faith a minute to think about it before she answered. "Almost three years now, I think. Trevor had a hard time getting Gabs to go out with him. She didn't want to get into anything to serious. Personally I think she wasn't quite over you yet, but Trevor was patient and waited until she was ready for something serious." Faith smiled while looking into the kitchen to see if the kettle was ready, it wasn't.

"So was Trevor your friend? Is that how they met."

"No Gabs introduced me to Trevor. She met him... somewhere it was nearly four years ago now, but he just seemed to fit right in with us."

Knox decided he didn't want to know any more about Trevor and to get to the reason for why he was there.

"Ah, Faith... what... um, can you tell me about what happened? When Gabs disappeared?" He sat silent while he watched Faith remember that day. Faith sat down on the couch across from Knox, closed her eyes trying to hold back the tears from remembering. Faith had always been an emotional person. Her friends always said it was what made her Faith, part of her charm. Faith gained control of her emotions and started telling Knox about that day.

"Not too much I'm afraid." Knox could hear the tears in her voice. "I came home from my E-Com class and saw the door was left open a bit. I thought Gabs had simply left the door open a crack for some airflow, it can get somewhat warm in here some days. So anyways I pushed the door open the rest of the way and called for Gabs but she didn't answer me."

"I went to her room to see if maybe she had fallen asleep but she wasn't there. I searched the rest of the apartment but obviously, as you can see it's not very big. I phoned Trevor to see if Gabs was with him but she wasn't."

"After that I thought maybe she went for a walk to clear her head or something. Gabs' is always going for walks when she's trying to work something out or if she's excited about something, for something; and always so late at night. I never understood her love of late night walks but she took them all the time. Anyways I waited for her to come home cause we had made plans to go out for dinner with Trevor and a few of our friends but she never come home, I phoned some of our friends to see if she was with any of them but she wasn't. That's when I phoned Doug at campus security to tell him something bad might have happened to Gabs. He calmed me down, said he'd keep a look out, see what he could find. He said he'd probably need some time. Exam time can be quite stressful you know. Anyways, after talking to Doug, I called Trevor again, just to see but nothing came of it. Trevor said she would show up when she was ready."

Knox sat nodding his head, listening to Faith when the kettle started to whistle, and startled Faith. She had forgotten all about putting the kettle on. Faith got up from the couch and headed back into the kitchen to take the kettle off.

After a couple of minutes, Faith came back with two cups of tea; she handed one to Knox then sat back down again. Faith slowly sipped at her hot tea looking down at the carpet trying to find where her thoughts were before being interrupted by the tea. When she remembered, Faith looked back up to Knox and continued on.

"So once I couldn't find Gabs and called everyone I could think of. I was super worried so I phoned the police to report a missing person. The person on the phone said a person had to be missing a full twenty-four hours before they can be declared officially missing and that if Gabs was still missing tomorrow to call back and they'd write it up. That made me mad, what a stupid rule! A full twenty-four hours and now it's been two weeks and nothing!" Faith was getting agitated at the thought of her friend still missing.

"After the full twenty four hours were up I phoned the police back and reported Gabs missing again. They sent some people down and I walked them through the day and then nothing. They figured she took off. Couldn't take college or something like that. I told the cops how Gabs was almost done school, and that she wouldn't leave with only a couple of months left. But they were jerks and I could tell they didn't really care and with no real evidence of a kidnapping, well..." Faith went silent thinking of her friend, wishing she'd walk in through the front door and act like the last two weeks were some big practical joke.

They were both silent as they drank more of their tea, Knox thinking through all the information he'd received throughout the day. Knox thought about asking Faith about the oily smudged print found on the door knob but remembered Doug saying there wasn't enough to get an I.D. off of it so that was also a dead end.

"Faith" Knox spoke breaking the silence, "Out of curiosity why did you wait so long to phone the Montgomery's."

Faith put her cup down and looked up to Knox. "I didn't want to worry them, I had hoped Gabs would only be missing for a couple of days, that someone would find her. But I knew after two weeks I had to tell them." Faith looked down at the carpet, the look of shame flashed across her pretty face, she knew she should have phoned John and Enid sooner, they had a right to know Gabriella was missing.

Knox could understand what Faith did and didn't blame her for not calling sooner, and he told her that.

"There's just... there's something I'd like to know if that's okay?" Knox asked Faith, she nodded curious about his question.

"Was... was Gabs happy? You know, before going missing. Was she happy?"

Faith smiled at his question, nodding her head. "Yes, Gabs is very happy."

Knox put his empty cup on the coffee table between the two couches. Looking at his watch Knox realized he had twenty minutes to get over to Dr. Beddingfeild's office. Dr. Wiseman had told Dr. Beddingfeild to expect Knox around one.

"Thank you Faith for the tea and telling me what you know about Gabs' disappearance. I have an appointment so I'm going to have to get going but if I need something or have more questions is it alright if I call or drop by?" Both Faith and Knox stood up as she replied.

"Yes, of course... oh before you go, I have a letter for you. I found it sitting on our kitchen counter the day she went missing. She must not have gotten to the post yet but since you're here, I'll just grab it." Faith grabbed the two photos' off the coffee table and vanished back onto Gabriella's room. Knox looked at his watch again, fifteen minutes until his meeting with Dr. Beddingfeild; Knox was glad his office was only a street away.

"Here." Faith said as she entered back into the living room handing Knox an envelope.

"Thanks." Knox took the envelope and stared down at Gabriella's writing on it. He desperately wanted to rip it open and learn its contents; but he knew now was not the time. After a small second, Knox slid the envelope into his inner coat pocket and headed for the door.

"Thank you again Faith."

"You, you will tell me if you find her... or find..."

"Yes, I will." Knox cut her off to answer then gave a small smile and walked out hearing Faith lock the door behind him

Chapter Twenty-One: Beddingfeild

Knox sat in Dr. Beddingfeild's waiting room grateful his office had only been a five-minute walk from Faith and Gabriella's apartment. Dr. Beddingfeild's waiting room was the complete opposite from Dr. Wiseman's. The walls were a bright sky blue with clouds painted randomly throughout the walls; he had two small evergreen coloured couches against the main wall with a small table with magazines on it.

All these things sat on dark hardwood flooring. On the other side of the room, there was a small wooden table with toys for children to play with. Knox was seated on one of the couches and grabbed the letter from his coat pocket. He glanced up to the clock on the wall telling him it was two minutes to one.

Knox figured he had time to read the letter, he opened it and just as he read his name at the top, the door to Dr. Beddingfeild's office opened and two people walked out. "Thank you Dr. Beddingfeild." A very skinny woman said sobbing as she turned from Dr. Beddingfeild and left.

"Yup, no problem; I'll see you next week Elaine." He smiled putting his hands into his dark blue jean pockets watching his patient leave the waiting room.

As Dr. Beddingfeild watched his patient leave, Knox placed the letter back into his pocket and stood up from the couch. When he looked up at Dr. Beddingfeild, he couldn't believe his eyes; it was the same man from the photo Faith had showed him earlier, it was Trevor.

Knox now looking at Trevor Beddingfeild fully found that his photo did not do him justice now. The handsome man he saw in the photo now looked ragged and run-down. As much as Knox was jealous of him, he couldn't help but feel bad at the same time. Trevor Beddingfeild stood 6'1" tall, lean and well-muscled, mid-thirties. His short wavy dirty-blond hair was in disarray; his bright blue eyes seemed as though they had not found sleep in days if not longer and his five o'clock shadow well passed in need of a shave. Trevor's attire was as ragged as he was; dark blue jeans and a wrinkled grey button down collared shirt.

Knox was a bit in shock and he could only imagine that the man's appearance was due to Gabriella's disappearance. Knox had not expected Gabriella's boyfriend to be the therapist Dr. Wiseman sent him too. He wondered about the ethics of their relationship only to quickly remember his own relationship with Gabriella was far from ethical.

"You must be Aidan Knox. I was told to expect you about this time." Trevor removed his hands from his pocket and offered Knox one. Knox took his hand and they both gave a very firm hand to each other; Knox's jealousy was in full bloom as he heard Trevor's thick British accent.

"Yes, Dr. Wiseman told you to expect me then." Knox replied as he dropped his grip allowing his hand to fall to his side.

"Yes... he did" Trevor said, "Please come in." Trevor turned into his office and Knox followed him in.

Trevor's office was large and homey. The walls where painted a tasteful light burgundy colour with the exception of the back right wall, which was brick. As Knox walked in he noticed the two couches matching the two out in the waiting room and a leather chair all turned into each other with a dark wooden coffee table in the middle.

Knox saw a large cabinet on the wall to the side of the circle of furniture. Trevor's desk sat in the upper left side of the office with piles of papers and books cluttering the surface. Across from his desk sat a small grand piano with some sheet music sitting on top. Trevor had bookshelves it seemed wherever he could put one overflowing, and had books strewn across his entire office.

Knox couldn't help but admire Trevor's office as he took a seat on one of the couches while Trevor sat in his leather chair. The two men sat in silence for a few moments. Knox tried to get a read on Trevor, trying to determine what kind of man he was, but he couldn't get a read on the run-down man before him.

Trevor broke the silence first, "So you're Aidan Knox. I must say it is nice to meet you. Gabs' has told me quite a bit about you; enough to make a man worried. She is quite fond of you, you know."

Knox could tell that Trevor was not as fond of him as Gabriella was. Knox had a feeling that under normal circumstances Trevor was actually a decent man but the stress of Gabriella's disappearance was making him curt.

Unfortunately, Trevor had to continue with his daily life, run his practice, see his patients and hope somehow, someone would find Gabriella.

"Gabriella told me people call you by your Last name." Trevor was attempting small talk.

"Gabs' mother preferred my last name to my first so she started to call me by it and it just sort of stuck. I like it. Sorry but you're not actually Gabs therapist are you? I saw Faith earlier today and she told me about you and Gabriella." Knox hadn't intended to blurt out that last part. But he decided it was best to lay everything out in the open and out of the way so he could get back to finding Gabriella. Knox took a deep breath and waited for Trevor's response.

"You're right, Gabs is not my patient and we are together as Faith told you. It took quite some time for Gabs and me to get where we are and now... and now she's missing... I can't even go and find her. I can't do anything to get her back. But let me ask you something Knox... what makes you think you can find her?"

Trevor showed a little more anger than he had meant to, lashing out at Knox. The two men just sat, half-glaring at each other, half feeling for the other. They both wanted the same thing, Gabriella back home and safe. Knox considered how to answer Trevor's question and decided to simply say what he believed so nice and calmly replied, "Because I know her better than anyone." He didn't smile, he didn't blink, he sat still, staring straight into Trevor's eyes and told it how it was. Trevor gave a small laugh, disagreeing with Knox's presumption.

"Do you disagree?" Knox's responded to Trevor's gesture.

"Oh no," Trevor started, "I can see why you would think that, I know your story Knox... Gabs told me how you were in love with her mother

Alice. How she turned you down and chose Gabs father instead of you. Gabs told me about your ex-wife, Grace, how you married her just so you wouldn't be alone, to hope that being with Grace would help you get over Alice. Then of course, Alice dies, Gabs father, Eli, loses his mind and tries to murder Gabs causing her to move to your little town, Babylon where she meets you. Gabs knew when the two of you were together in the beginning that you were only with her to try to be with Alice. But of course, like most of us, you fell in love with her. I can't blame you; she's hard not to love. Even with all her semi-crazy quirks and bad habits.

"But here's the thing Knox. Yes, you have a lot of history with Gabs and her family, but that doesn't mean you know her better than anyone else. Where have you been these last four years? I know where I've been, I've been here with Gabs, seeing how college changed her, watching her get over you, which let me tell you took a long time. She is not the girl you knew; just remember that while you search for her. Moreover, ask yourself why? Do you think you'll play he hero and she'll go back to you? Because even if you find her; I don't see that happening."

Trevor was a rock, solid; he allowed his anger and resentment for Knox combined with his anxiety for Gabriella too completely consume him. When either of them spoke, it was quite clear to the other that they were not going to get along.

Knox found it hard to look Trevor in the eye, so he let his eyes wander over the room. Knox's eyes stopped on the piano and noticed a guitar behind it. It was Gabriella's. Trevor, curious to know what caught Knox's eyes, followed his gaze over the instruments and he spoke again, hoping their next attempt at conversation would go a bit better, calmer.

"I think that's one of the things I miss the most about Gabs. I miss her music. She has such a way about it, how she writes. She has one of the most amazing voices I've ever heard." Trevor noticed Knox's eyes shot back over to him and Trevor realized this conversation probably wasn't going to go over any better than the previous.

"She... she plays for you?" It wasn't so much a question as a shocking statement for Knox. He knew how private Gabriella was with her music. Trevor could see how uncomfortable that notion made Knox.

"Yes Gabs plays for me. We play together quite a lot." Trevor had a small smile on his face as he remembered playing with Gabriella.

Knox was still confused on a few things about Trevor, about Gabriella; what confused him the most was how they became an item. Dr. Wiseman had sent Gabriella to Trevor for counseling and therapy not a new boyfriend. Knox decided seeing how they weren't exactly holding back the shots on each other to simply ask and clear up his confusion.

"Sorry Beddingfeild, but I'm confused on how this all happened. You and Gabriella, to my understanding Dr. Wiseman sent Gabs to you so she could continue on with her therapy not..." Knox had to stop himself before he said something uncalled for. Luckily, for Knox, Trevor understood what he was getting at. So Trevor put his other emotions aside for a moment and gave Knox a calm and professional answer, also hoping that by clearing up any confusion the two of them might actually be able to work together and possibly get Gabriella back.

"Knox look four years ago when I met Gabriella, and you're right, Robert sent her to me for professional help and for those first couple sessions we talked about her childhood, her life in Babylon. She spoke a great amount about you. Gabriella would tell me how much she missed you; she struggled with the idea of dropping out and going back to Babylon but over time she found just how much she loved being here.

"The experience of college, she managed to make a couple of really good friends, like Faith. It wasn't an easy task for Gabs, she's really quite shy, and as for the music, well that only started about a year and a half ago. That's when she finally let me hear her. I found that what Gabriella really need was a friend. Someone to confide in as she had with you and David but she needed a bit more than she had, she needed someone to trust and help her adjust to her new life. Being somewhere new and alone was hard for Gabriella so instead of becoming her new therapist I became her friend. I think the first two or three times Gabriella came here, it was professional but that really wasn't what she needed and we spoke about all this. Gabriella didn't want me out of her life nor I her, so we became friends and over time we did become more. And I just want you to know that I love her, more than anything and I am just as worried and scared for her as you are. The only difference is I don't have the luxury to drop my life and go find her. God, I wish I could, but my patients need me."

Trevor gave Knox a lot to chew on, and could see that Knox was still taking everything in.

"She's not the same Gabs I knew and loved is she?" Knox was talking to himself but Trevor answered him anyway.

"People change Knox and it's been years since you've been Gabriella's. She's changed just in my time of knowing her. The same thing could hold true for you as well. Are you the same man you were four years ago?" It was more of a rhetorical question and Trevor could see that Knox agreed with him. "You're still in love with her, aren't you?" Trevor knew the answer but he felt the needed to hear it anyways.

Knox took a breath then answered, "I never stopped, but then I did love her long before I knew her." Knox had decided that like Trevor he had to put his jealousy and dislike aside. Both men had stopped attacking each other and accepted that for the time being they needed to be able to work together.

Both men sat in silence again; they were beginning to understand each other. Trevor broke the silence first. "Can I ask... ah... how often did Gabs sing and play for you?" Trevor decided he wanted to know a bit more about him and Gabriella.

"Uhm..." Knox was a bit taken aback by Trevor's question; unsure why or where he was planning to take this conversation, "Not very often... like you said Gabs, well she's very shy, especially when it comes to her music. I did manage to get her to sing once in class but I only heard her couple of times after that."

"You're not musically inclined then?"

"Ah, no... I'm more philosophical than musical... I thought Gabs was too but—"

"Oh no, she is, Gabs has a real passion for literature," Trevor jumped in when Knox took a pause. "But music, I mean she is truly gifted and it's really something to watch her play. It's as if you can see right into her soul. It really is one of the most beautiful thing I have had the privilege of seeing." Trevor wanted Knox to know that there's a lot more to Gabriella than perhaps he thought.

"She never wanted to explore music. She never mentioned or said anything, I mean at most she would sing along with the radio but that was it." Knox didn't like where this conversation had gone, it was causing him to question how well he actually knew Gabriella; he wondered what else she had kept from him. As much as Knox hated to admit that Trevor was right, he was.

Knox hadn't been with Gabriella for four years; sure they sent letters and kept in touch, saw each other over Christmas and a week or two during the summer but that's not being with someone. Knox had to accept that Gabriella might have found something better for herself in GreenBay.

Trevor could see Knox's mind was going through, thought after thought and he decided to interrupt his thought process.

"Would you like to see her Knox?"

"Wait, what?" Knox shot straight up, very confused by what he had just heard. "I thought you didn't know where she was." Trevor immediately understood Knox's anxiety and corrected his statement as Knox sat back down.

"Sorry, I don't know where she is. What I meant was would you like to see her video? We recorded ourselves playing; I thought you might like to see her play." Trevor didn't have to wait to know Knox's answer. He could tell Knox wanted to see it and so as Knox was nodding and saying 'Yes' Trevor stood from his leather chair and moved over to the large oak cabinet and opened the doors, showing a 36' TV and a DVD player. On the right side of the cabinet Trevor had, a CD rack filled with CDs and DVDs. Trevor grabbed a DVD on the top shelf and put it into the DVD player.

Trevor turned everything on and went back to his chair. "I've watched this quite a bit since she's gone missing." Trevor admitted.

"Does Gabriella know you have this?" Knox was concerned about her privacy.

"Oh yes, this was her idea. Mine was to simply record us on the computer but she liked the idea of being able to watch them years later, so we made a DVD." Trevor could tell that Knox was starting to get overwhelmed by everything but truly believed that the video would make him feel better. Trevor pressed play and they both focused on the TV.

"Do you have it?" Trevor was sitting at the piano, calling out to Gabriella.

"Hold on, I'm getting there, Just making sure you're centered. The Camera loves you by the way." Gabriella had a laugh in her voice as she shifted the camera back and forth. "Okay, I got it, perfect."

The camera had finally stopped moving and Trevor was in the center of the screen. Trevor's eyes moved with Gabriella as she cut in front of the camera to go stand behind him. As Gabriella stood behind Trevor she leaned into him, wrapping her arms around his neck, letting her arms fall down his chest, giving him a half hug while kissing him gently on the cheek. Both of them are smiling and happy while Trevor leans back into Gabriella happily accepting her.

Trevor gently starts to play the piano and quietly hums along as Gabriella keeps hold of him, her eyes closed, lightly swaying with Trevor as he plays. After a moment, Gabriella releases Trevor and grabs her guitar sitting behind them. She pulls the strap over her head so the guitar is sitting against her chest. Trevor continues his melody while Gabriella starts to strum lightly, matching the melody.

They play four bars before Gabriella starts to sing.

'I can see the sadness in your eyes
I can see the pain within your soul
I know the tears of your heart, yeah, oh'

Trevor came in on the chorus.

'Cause we're all broken
Our souls are in two
Yeah we're all broken
But we pulled through
Oh we're all broken
But I'll keep loving you
Will you love me too?'

Gabriella stopped singing, allowing Trevor to have the second verse.

'You try and hid all that you are

Hoping no one will see you
You've seen some demons In your time yeah
Well honey so have I, Oh.

Gabriella came in for the chorus

'Cause we're all broken
Our souls are in two
Yeah we're all broken
But we pulled through
Oh we're all broken
But I'll keep loving you
Will you love me too?'

Trevor finished the melody transitioning into another one as Gabriella set her guitar back down and sat next to Trevor.

Chapter Twenty-Two: Exchange

Knox was sitting on his motel bed going through everything in his mind. He had ruled out the possibility of a stranger having her, so he started to think of everyone he knew who would be capable of taking her, who would have a reason. Knox would have liked Trevor for it, but only because he was involved with her. However, he knew it wasn't Trevor. Knox couldn't help but wonder if Dr. Wiseman knew about Gabriella and Trevor.

It was still early so Knox decided to call Dr. Wiseman and find out if he deliberately let him get bombarded with that news.

The phone rang a few times before Dr. Wiseman answered.

"Hello."

"Hi, it's Knox."

"Knox how are things going? Any closer to finding Gabriella?"

"Ah, no, not yet, Um, actually, I had a question for you, about your friend, Trevor, and Gabriella." There was a pause on the other side of the line, so Knox continued.

"Did you know that they're a couple?"

"Yes I knew."

"Then Why? Why did you send me to him without telling me? Why did you have me believe that he was her therapist?" Knox was angry, but tried to keep his temper as Dr. Wiseman responded.

"Knox, would you have gone if you knew that she was seeing someone? That she had moved on? Honestly, you needed to know and

161

I couldn't tell you. You had to find out on your own. So it wouldn't stop you from trying to find Gabriella. You have to remember that none of this is about you, it's all about her, finding her, and nothing else matters right now." The line went silent again. Knox agreed with Dr. Wiseman in his head. "So do you want to tell me what else you've learned Knox?" Dr. Wiseman wanted to move off the subject and get on to what he felt was more important now.

"Beddingfeild, maybe did it?" Knox was only half kidding as he said it.

"Knox." Dr. Wiseman chided.

"Alright, alright, I know it's not him. Well I haven't learned that much. The police aren't that much help and the campus security has their hands tied. They've done everything they can. You know I don't believe some random person did this, and if she was taken for a ransom then why, after two weeks why has no one been contacted? I do believe that she knew her abductor, whoever has her, wanted her, I just don't know what for. I don't think she's dead or someone would've found her by now. None of this makes sense. I have no proof, no evidence, just theories. I mean, Gabs wouldn't have dropped out and left, not with so little time left in school. I... just... what do you think?"

"Well, I agree that this was not random and that Gabriella didn't run off, that's just not her. As to who took her, who's capable, I can't tell you. I can tell you that yes; she most likely knew her abductor. They had most likely been stalking her for a while, and then they snapped. Something would have triggered that person to go from stalking to actual kidnapping. Most typical in these circumstances is an ex or someone like that but as we both know Gabriella doesn't have many ex's and I hardly think it's you so it's a good chance it's someone she met at school. There must be something we're not seeing."

"I... I don't know; Doug from campus security says Gabriella is the only student missing and the only other person unaccounted for right now is a teacher oh... what's his name?"

Dr. Wiseman cut Knox off while he was searching for the name. "Well was there a connection between Gabriella's disappearance and this missing teacher?"

"Kenneth Madson, that's his name and Um... Gabriella took most of his classes and ah... yeah they were friends. Do you think he might have taken her? Maybe he liked her, wanted more than a friendship, and got jealous about Beddingfeild? No, no that doesn't make sense. Doug said they were never anything more than just friends." Knox was rambling over the phone, trying to put all the pieces together. Dr. Wiseman cut off his rambling.

"No, I don't believe Kenneth would take Gabriella, she spoke of him, and he's a good man, according to Gabriella. Their friendship was platonic. Did you say he went missing around the same time?"

"Ah, yeah, that's what Doug said."

"Then perhaps who ever took Gabriella took Kenneth as well." Dr. Wiseman fell silent to let Knox determine the possibility. After a moment Knox finally spoke, trying to keep his rambling at bay.

"That's a possibility but where's the motive? Why take them both? Is there something only they can do or..." Knox's mind was starting to go off again.

"Knox." Dr. Wiseman was trying to get his attention again.

"Knox."

"Yeah, sorry, I just can't make sense of any of this. Gabriella goes missing along with her teacher? Why?"

"Perhaps the kidnapper got jealous of the wrong man?" Dr. Wiseman was trying to make as much sense of this as Knox.

Knox was pondering that thought, it's plausible if Gabriella spent enough time with Kenneth, their abductor could have misjudged. Dr. Wiseman believed himself to be right.

"So where do I go from here? Now what? I'm still no closer to actually finding Gabs and..." Knox was at a complete loss and had no clue what his next step should be.

"I don't know." Was the only thing Dr. Wiseman could say; He had no more help for Knox.

"Yeah, well, thanks." And Knox hung up the phone.

Knox's mind was still racing with ideas and possibilities on who took Gabriella. He sat up more on the hard motel bed and stared at the black TV that was turned off across from him. After a moment of silence, Knox went over to the desk where his bag sat and grabbed a notebook out of it. He then moved back to the bed, grabbing a pen just before settling back down. He started to write down everything he had learned.

Chapter Twenty-Three: Progress

Knox woke the next morning a bit disoriented; he hadn't slept well and when he looked over at the clock by the TV; it read twenty to ten. He sat upright in bed only to see paper's surrounding him and a bottle of Scotch almost completely empty. Knox had hoped that everything had just been a bad dream. That none of it had happened. For most of the night Knox remembered the last time he was in a motel, he was with Gabriella, he had finally told her just how much he loved her, and she told him she was leaving him, moving and going to GreenBay College. It was both the happiest and saddest night of his life. Knox's head was still a bit foggy from the scotch the night before so he decided to stay in bed until his head straightened out.

When Knox woke up the second time, it was almost noon. He felt a bit better, his hangover had dissipated and he managed to get up and shower. The cold fact of the day still haunted him, he knew was he was no closer to Gabriella and wondered if he'd ever actually find her or if he was just on some wild goose chase with no happy ending.

It was a bit before one when there was a knock on Knox's motel room door. Knox went to answer the door but whoever knocked had left. There was an envelope with his name on it sitting on the ground in front of the door. Knox grabbed the envelope and went back into his motel room. He looked at the envelope with great curiosity, wondering who would leave him something. Knox sat back down on the bed with the mess of papers and opened the envelope; he took out the note and read:

'GO HOME, YOU WON'T FIND HER. SHE'S MINE.
STOP BEFORE SOMEONE ELSE GETS HURT.'

Knox just sat and stared at the note, shocked. Someone knew he was looking. The note finally gave Knox the proof that someone took Gabriella; the note also told Knox that whoever took her was afraid he'd get too close, after a couple more reads of the note Knox called Trevor to let him know about it, to get his impression of his new threatening note. Trevor asked Knox to come back to his office around two o'clock to go over everything and try to come up with a next step. Knox had about an hour before meeting Trevor so he spent his time gathering up his mess of paper and re-reading the note repeatedly. Knox found something familiar about it but he couldn't put his finger on it.

At two o'clock Knox was once again sitting in Trevor's waiting room. Trevor didn't keep Knox waiting long, he was very anxious to see the note Knox had received. Trevor read the note a good dozen times, trying to make sense of why it was sent.

"You have no idea who sent it?" Trevor asked.

"No."

"Have you taken it to the police?" Trevor asked while waving the note in front of Knox.

"No."

Trevor was trying to stay calm with what the note stated. He agreed with Knox that whoever had Gabriella was watching him and was afraid Knox would get too close. Trevor did not respond well to the note reference of Gabriella being her abductors and both men wondered who had been hurt already hoping it wasn't Gabriella and curious if it was Kenneth Madson; if he was with her. They agreed not to inform the police about the note figuring they still wouldn't do anything useful. Trevor looked through all the notes Knox had written, trying to make sense of the connections Knox had tried to make.

"Knox, what do you think he meant when he said she's his now. That rather proves that Gabs knows who took her. Someone from her past makes the most sense to me; I know most of the people she sees since she started school." Trevor was mostly thinking aloud, hoping something would click.

"I've thought of that, but I'm at a loss as to whom. I'm trying to figure out who would want her this badly." Knox replied anyways.

"Okay… let's try and break this down, who in her past could want Gabriella so much they would resort to kidnapping? How about her father Eli? He did try to murder her as a kid. I don't think it'd be a bad idea to look into him as an option. Do you?"

Knox started to mentally kick himself for not thinking about Eli earlier; he had completely forgotten about him.

"No, I hadn't, he didn't even cross my mind, and last I heard he was still locked up at the Ridgefield Mental Institution."

"Well let's make sure he's still there then." Trevor stood from his leather chair and moved over to his desk. He grabbed his address book and flipped through until he found the number for Ridgefield. Knox had followed Trevor over to his desk and sat in one of the chairs in front watching Trevor dial the number. Knox could only hear Trevor's side of the call. "Hi this is Dr. Trevor Beddingfeild and I'm calling to inquire after a patient."

"That's right I'm a psychotherapist over in GreenBay."

"Eli Harris." Pause.

"It's regarding his daughter actually, what do you mean you have no information on him." Another pause.

"Then get me someone who has infor—" He was cut off.

"Alright, I understand, I do but this is important." Pause again.

"Just… can you at least tell me if Eli Harris is there?" Pause.

"I just want to know if he is in the building." Pause.

"Yes, I understand that you cannot release patient information unless okayed by a family member, however…"

"Alright, then will you at least tell me who's treating him or better yet let me speak to him, it is quite important." Pause.

"I didn't ask if he was busy. I asked to speak to him, I figured he's busy."

That was the end of the phone call. Trevor sat down into his desk chair while Knox sat across from him, arms folded over his chest.

"So I guess that didn't go well then?"

Trevor could hear the sarcasm in Knox's voice and he just looked at him, annoyed.

"No, it didn't. That woman wouldn't even put me through to Eli's Doctor."

"Did you at least get the Doctor's name?"

"Oh Yeah, it's Dr. Fredrick Holmes. I've heard of him, he's supposed to be one of the best in the field."

The two of them sat in glum silence, trying to decide on their next move. Trevor broke the silence first.

"How much time were you able to get off of work?" Trevor was trying to determine how much time he was going to give to his search for Gabriella.

"Ah, well, at least a couple of weeks. I'm hoping it won't take that long, but I'm sure I could take more time if I need to, why?"

"Oh, just curious."

"Well... now what?"

"I don't know but I would like to know if Eli is actually at Ridgefield though."

"Yeah, so would I."

They both fell silent thinking the same thing and the looks were passing. They knew they were sharing the same thought. Someone needed to drive up to Ridgefield and make sure Eli was there. Again, Trevor broke the silence in the room.

"So you can't get into Ridgefield. You do know that right?" Trevor decided that blunt and obvious would be the best way to take the conversation.

"Yes, but you can."

"Yes, as a psychotherapist I'm able to get in. I can say I'm looking to admit a patient, ask to talk to Dr. Holmes. I'm sure I can clear my schedule for a day and go up. And—" Knox cut Trevor off.

"Hold on, I want to go too. Hear what Dr. Holmes has to say."

"You want to go? And how would you get in?"

"Yes, look I don't want to miss anything and if this Dr. Holmes can give us anything useful then I want... I should be there. And I don't know, I can be a family member of the 'patient' you're thinking of admitting." As much as Trevor hated to admit it, he thought Knox's idea might actually work.

"Alright that might work Knox; we can go tomorrow around nine. That should give enough time to cancel all my patients. You're staying at the GreenBay Motel off the highway right?"

"Yeah"

"Okay I'll be there at nine to pick you up then." Trevor rose from his office chair and headed back to his coffee table by the chair and couches to start cleaning up the mess of papers. Knox followed and helped collect all the paper he had brought with him.

Trevor and Knox worked out a few last minute details for their outing tomorrow before Knox left to go check in on Faith before calling it a day.

Chapter Twenty-Four: Ridgefield

Knox hardly slept that night, laying in his motel bed playing out scenarios in his head on how the following day would go; thinking on what to do if Eli was there, if he wasn't, thinking and remembering Gabriella. By the time the clock read 7:00 Knox gave up completely on sleep and driving himself crazy thinking about past happiness and the day ahead; he climbed out of bed and headed for the shower, deciding to get ready for the day. Knox was getting used to the restless nights worrying about Gabriella, trying to find a way to get her back.

Once Knox was ready, he still had just over an hour before Trevor would be there. Knox sat on the bed reading his notes again trying to find any lead to Gabriella.

Trevor was at his door right at nine, holding coffees and an envelope. "This was at your door." Trevor said while handing Knox the envelope and one of the coffees.

"Oh." Knox took a coffee and the envelope, set the coffee on the counter to open and read what was inside.

'GO HOME.
LAST WARNING KNOX,
FORGET HER, SHE'S MINE.'

Under the note was a picture of a dead man with the words:

'NO ONE ELSE HAS TO DIE
YOU'VE BEEN WARNED.'

The note was written all in capital letters with a black sharpie.

Knox froze; it was not what he was expecting to see first thing in the morning. He passed the note and the photo to Trevor to show him. "It's another one, but worse." Knox said as he handed Trevor everything.

Trevor was silent for a few moments, taking in the note and photo. "That's Kenneth Madson." Trevor managed to get out after processing the photo, "He was a good man."

Trevor handed the note and photo back to Knox; he didn't want to see it anymore. He was friends with Kenneth; Kenneth was a part of their small group. Gabriella, Trevor, Faith, and Kenneth would get together all the time. It hurt Trevor to see how his friend ended.

"We... we should get going." Trevor turned and headed out to his car. Knox grabbed his coffee and jacket closing the door behind him as he followed Trevor out.

Knox decided to remain silent for a bit once they got on the road giving Trevor time to come to terms with the loss of his friend.

Knox knew that Gabriella was still alive, the notes, he'd been given told him that, he felt for Kenneth, thinking he simply got caught up in all the madness by mistake.

"Do you think Eli is capable of all this?" Trevor finally broke the silence.

"Well he did try to murder his daughter in the past; I wouldn't put anything past Eli. I have no doubt he's capable of just about anything." Knox and Trevor exchanged a look that showed they were both afraid of how everything might end.

"She's not dead, we know that. We just have to find her. She's not dead." Trevor was speaking aloud, mostly trying to comfort himself.

"You really love her, don't you? And miss her. I can see it; it's in your eyes." Knox wasn't sure why he said it, maybe to simply have it said.

"So do you though."

Knox didn't respond to Trevor's last comment, she knew he was right, but it was something, neither of them could do anything about.

Neither Knox nor Trevor was sure what they were expecting to find at Ridgefield, they had never been before. Trevor had read about the facility, how it's said to be one of the best in the country, highly recommended. The patients were well-treated and looked after, given ample amount of attention; family and friends were welcome to visit.

Trevor had decided to change his approach to getting in. He would go in being a friend of Eli Harris thinking they would automatically confirm him being there or not.

Knox was surprised when he realized they were there already, but then he had been so wrapped up in his little thoughts he would have little attention for the two hour drive they were on. Trevor pulled up to the front gate and rolled down his window to show his ID to the guard.

"Hello." Trevor spoke in his normal, happy, outgoing voice, while giving the guard his ID. "How's it going?" He tried to make small talk but the guard wasn't engaging him. The guard asked what their business was and Trevor told him they were coming to expect the facility because he was admitting a patient here. The guard handed back the ID and waved them through.

"What was that?" Knox had stayed quiet, allowing Trevor to handle the guard but he went back to his original plan, which confused him.

"I thought with the guard that would be easier. He couldn't really argue with the purpose could he? I am a doctor and doctor's go to places like this all the time to make arrangements for their patients."

"Right" Was the only response Knox could come up with.

The drive up to the main building only took a couple of minutes and Trevor was able to find a spot to park within minutes. The pair of them sat in the car a few minutes longer, staring up at the huge mansion size building.

"Okay; how exactly do you intend to get us in there then Trevor?"

"Well how about Gabriella hired us to be her father's new doctors? How does that sound? Or we're family friends?"

"Well Eli believes I ruined his marriage, causing Alice to commit suicide and you're seeing his daughter... I don't think we can go in as family friends."

"Good point, Doctor's then?"

"Doctor's it is. Good thing you are one."

"Yeah, so we're not completely lying… just mostly."

"Well mostly lying is better than fully lying. So do you think it will work, saying Gabriella hired us?"

"Yeah… sure" Trevor didn't sound very convincing, but he wasn't giving Knox much of a choice on the matter. He unbuckled his seat belt and stepped out of the car, heading up to the front door with Knox following beside him.

Knox stayed just behind Trevor, allowing him to lead and take point. He didn't love their plan but had little say in it at any point. As they stepped up the large cement steps up to the metal barred doors. Knox noticed how the whole place was giving him a creepy feel, as if he'd just stepped into a horror movie when they go to look for someone in the big haunted castle and when they step inside the place is old and dusty, large rooms leading God knows where. Then someone decides to split up to find who they're look for only for them all to be killed off one by one.

Knox decided he needed to stop watching horror movies, and hoped they wouldn't have to stay too long.

Trevor led the way inside and up to reception desk. Knox noticed that being in the institution didn't seem to bother Trevor too much. Knox figured it was because Trevor was so used to being around the mentally unstable.

Knox however was surprised by the place, he was creped out for sure but the place was not as dark and dingy as he had imagined it to be. The institution was clean and light. The floor was cement but the walls were all nicely painted beige colour.

Trevor was chatting up the young woman working the desk trying to get access to Eli Harris. Trevor showed her his ID proving he was who he was claiming to be while giving her his nicest smile; charming her with his English accent, watching her go all school girl crush on him and with that she let them through. Trevor walked away from the desk back over to Knox with a 'we're in' smile.

"Well, he's here which means he doesn't have Gabs. But Mindy, the receptionist is going to let us in to talk to him."

"Alright, but if he's here and doesn't have her, he probably has no clue that she's even missing. He can't help us Trevor."

Trevor could see the struggle in Knox and understood it.

"Look, as unpleasant as this may be, we've got to talk to him. The fact that Eli is here is a very good thing. It means he doesn't have Gabs, I mean, think of what she might have gone through again if Eli had her."

"I don't want to think about what might be happening to her in any case.

The men headed down the hallway reaching another metal door waiting to get buzzed through. Knox stayed just behind Trevor again, and he knew his question might be redundant but he had to ask it anyways.

"Okay, we know that Eli is here and does not have Gabriella... then why are we talking to him?"

Trevor could tell Knox was creped out and that he desperately wanted to leave. He almost found it amusing; Trevor always got a kick out of newbie's coming into Mental Institutions, but Trevor found Knox's discomfort slightly more amusing than he should have. He figured it was because Knox was Gabriella's ex.

"Well, I did ask to see him, and it would raise some suspicion if we didn't see him after asking to. Don't worry, it shouldn't take very long." Trevor tried to give a reassuring smile.

Trevor's reason seemed reasonable enough to Knox. He still didn't like it but there was nothing he could do. Knox remembered what Eli was like before his mental break down; he didn't particularly want to see Eli now that he was insane. As it was, Knox was hardly Eli's favourite person in the world; and even after everything Eli blamed Knox for his wife's suicide so he wasn't sure how well Eli would take to seeing him.

They came to the end of the long corridor and waited to get buzzed through another door. When they entered they could see Eli sitting at the table doing a puzzle by himself. The room was full of patients and employees of the facility; everyone seemed to be doing something. There was a group sitting in front of the TV, watching some old black and white movie. Some were engaged in conversation, some were sitting around a table playing cards while some simply watched others play the card games. Nurses were walking around, making sure everyone was behaving and that order was being maintained.

Trevor wasn't overwhelmed by the events going on in the room unlike Knox whose eyes were looking everywhere. He was fascinated by everything that was going on, it was a completely new experience for him. So different from his classroom which he quickly began to miss.

Trevor and Knox were standing off to the side of the doorway taking in the feel of the room. Trevor kept his attention on Eli sitting alone quietly doing his puzzle. He took notice how some of the patients were deliberately staying away, but always keeping an eye on him. Trevor got the impression that most of the patients were afraid of him.

Trevor glanced at Knox, making sure he was handling everything all right, and then the two of them headed over to Eli. Trevor was prepared to go right up to Eli but his path got cut off by a bear of a man wearing a wrinkled grey suit; he looked overworked and very tired. Just by looking at him, you knew the institution was his life and that it was wearing him out.

"Dr. Beddingfeild." The bear of a man walked straight up to Trevor and Knox, stretching out his hand for Trevor to shake.

"Dr. Holmes I take it?" Trevor took his hand as the two men greeted each other.

"Yes, it's nice to meet you; so dear Gabriella decided to get a second opinion has she."

"No she hasn't actually." Dr. Holmes looked confused, as did Knox. Trevor was not following their plan. Trevor continued to speak. "Gabriella has gone missing and we thought perhaps Eli had taken her. We came here to make sure he was actually here. But clearly he is and we will have to find another way of finding her."

Dr. Holmes stood there nodding his head up and down, while Knox was trying to understand why he decided to confess instead of sticking to their plan. Dr. Holmes broke Knox's train of thought when he spoke.

"Gabriella's missing. I do hope she's all right, such a nice young woman, so sweet. Well of course feel free to talk to Eli, not sure what help he'll be but go ahead." Dr. Holmes realized he said something, which shocked both Trevor and Knox.

"What?"

It took a minute for Trevor to find his words while Knox was waiting to ask the question they were both thinking.

"Sorry, but you know Gabriella?" Knox got the question out before Trevor could.

"Yes, she comes in to visit Eli." Dr. Holmes was trying to understand their confusion.

"She visits Eli? How... how long has she been doing that? When was the last time she was here?" Trevor was asking the questions this time.

"Oh, well she comes once a month, normally the first Saturday of the month to visit Eli and she's been doing so for... when let's see... well at least this last year and a half but before then she'd drop in sporadically for a couple of years. Didn't you know?"

Trevor and Knox were dumbfounded; they had no idea that Gabriella visited. They thought she didn't associate with him, with their history, they didn't think she'd want to.

"Ah, I... we had no idea... um, with their history well..." Dr. Holmes cut Trevor off.

"Yes, well that took a while but they've made a lot of progress. Eli is still a bit unstable so he's watched closely. Especially when Gabriella is here but progress is being made. Oh and we haven't seen her since last month. She never came this month but now I know why."

"Yes, she's been missing for about two weeks now. And if you're sure you're alright with us talking to Eli. I'm sure we'll only be a few minutes."

"Oh, sure, no problem Dr. Beddingfeild, take your time." They shook hands again, and then Dr. Holmes shook Knox's hand and then carried on with his days' work.

Trevor gave a slight chuckle then said, "Even missing she's still able to surprise me." He chuckled again then headed over to Eli with Knox right behind him silently laughing at Trevor's statement because he was thinking the same thing.

They walked the short distance to where Eli was sitting. Eli didn't look up from his puzzle. He was focused on trying to finish the roof of his cottage. Trevor and Knox stood for a second, watching Eli placing his puzzle piece. Once his piece was in place, Trevor gently cleared his throat to get Eli's attention. When that didn't work, he actually said his name, sitting down at Eli's puzzle table.

"Are you a new doctor?" Eli's voice was harsh, bitter, and course; how a voice would sound after years of smoking, "Come to examine the crazy man?" Eli still kept his eyes on his puzzle, thinking about his next piece.

Eli was a thin man, sickly looking from his years of smoking, drugs and alcohol. His hair had grown thin and grey, glasses sliding off his nose.

Knox decided Trevor wasn't going to be able to get Eli's full attention, so he spoke up.

"Eli."

"Oh I recognize that Scottish accent." Eli finally looked up from his puzzle and stared right at Knox as he mimicked his accent as he said Scottish. "The Scotsman," Eli continued, "Who ruined my life. Tell me now, my wife wasn't enough, you had to have my daughter too?" Eli had a small grim on his face as he spoke, as hatred ran through his course voice.

"I didn't ruin your life Eli; you did that all on your own."

"No oh no. I'm not the one that confused Alice's mind. She didn't kill herself because of me. It was you. You should have stayed away once you found out we were getting married, everything would have been fine if you hadn't confused her about me."

"Eli did you ever stop and think that maybe Alice simply saw you for who you really are, or were? Her death is not on my hands Eli." Trevor decided it would be a good time to step in.

"Um... Eli what, ah, Gabriella, she comes to visit you?"

"Yeah, so what of it?"

"Well, she's gone missing. You wouldn't know anything about that, would you?"

"Why don't you ask Mr. Scotsman there? From what I understand, he likes to keep an eye on my girl. Who are you anyways?" Eli finally took his eyes off Knox and transferred them to Trevor.

"I'm Trevor Beddingfeild, your daughter's friend."

"You mean her boyfriend. Yeah, she told me all about you."

"I wasn't sure."

"No, she likes you. Says you're great, and quite the piano player or whatever you guys are called."

"Pianist"

"Yeah, that's the word. Anyways, she talks about you."

"Well sorry if I seem a bit surprised. I had no idea Gabs was coming to see you."

"Well, that's not surprising. My girl has many secrets. Always has. Sorry I can't help you find her. I hope you find her, I missed her this month, she's all I've got left." Eli looked sad at the idea of losing his only outside connection.

"Thank you Eli... I'll let you know if we find her."

"No need. If you find her, she'll come back." Eli dropped his eyes back to his puzzle. Trevor couldn't help but feel for him, the amount of faith and hope he had for his daughter. It was not what he had expected to find and Knox was just as surprised. The two stood up and walked away leaving Eli to his solitude.

Knox and Trevor were silent as they walked out of the Ridgefield Mental Institution. The pair of them we're going over the day's events over and over again in their minds. Both given much more to think about then they thought they would.

Chapter Twenty-Five: Betrayal

The drive back to GreenBay was long and silent. Knox and Trevor didn't say two words to each other and avoided all eye contact when possible. They were both thinking of Gabriella, and what else she might be keeping to herself.

It was about six o'clock when Trevor and Knox got back into GreenBay and at Trevor's office. They needed to come up with a new plan in finding Gabriella along with dealing with the notes and photo Knox had been sent.

Trevor went to unlock his door discovering someone already unlocked it. Trevor stood in front of his door. It was slightly open; Knox came to see what Trevor was staring at. They knew they'd have to go inside. Trevor looked over at Knox, then took a deep breath to calm his nerves and pushed the door open the rest of the way; walking into his office with extreme caution.

Knox entered after Trevor curious to what they would find. Knox went and stood next to Trevor who was in front of his coffee table. Knox looked down at what Trevor was staring at. It was a picture of Gabriella, beaten, with another note attached to it. Knox reached down and pulled the note off the photo of Gabriella.

'You had no business at
Ridgefield today. Her beating
is on the two of you. Forget

about Gabriella or you will
both end up like Kenneth Madson.'

Knox handed the note to Trevor so he could read it and looked at the large photo of Gabriella again. Trevor tossed the note on the table and said, "Someone's watching us."

Knox nodded his head in agreement, as he stared at the note Trevor had tossed down. There was something familiar about the note. He pulled the other two notes out of his jacket pocket and looked at them. There was something, Knox just couldn't put his finger on.

Trevor turned his attention to Knox and of the picture of Gabriella curious why he was comparing the notes.

"What is it?" Trevor asked.

"I recognize the writing." Knox looked over at Trevor. "I just... it's so familiar." Knox was getting frustrated over the handwriting. He knew it, had seen it somewhere before. He looked at the new note and it was as if a light had turned on. "Is that a stain?"

Knox looked closer at the note, and in the bottom, right corner there was some sort of residue. He handed it to Trevor and checked the other two notes.

"It looks like an oil stain of some sort." Trevor confirmed what Knox was thinking.

"Look at these two as well." Knox handed the other two notes to Trevor and sure enough in the bottom, right corner was an oil stain.

"It's just a couple of stains, what's the big deal?" Trevor was trying to understand the importance of an oil stain.

"Would you say that's motor oil?" Trevor looked at the stain again but a bit closer this time and shrugged his shoulders.

"Could be, why?" Trevor watched Knox becoming concerned. Knox was shaking his head as though he was yelling at himself.

"Knox, do you want to fill me in here?" Trevor was getting anxious; Knox had clearly figured something out.

"That bastard! That son of a bitch!" Knox yelled out, confusing Trevor even more.

"What?" Trevor started to ask before Knox started going off again.

"The little shit." Then he turned to Trevor, "Come on, we've got to go." Knox turned and left Trevor's office with Trevor close behind him, confused about what had just happened.

Chapter Twenty-Six: Gabriella

Knox wasted no time, they went to his motel room and grabbed all of his things, then quickly hit the highway, heading back to Babylon. Trevor was still confused and Knox tried to explain everything but he was consumed with rage, worried about where he now knew Gabriella to be. Trevor tried to get Knox to slow down a bit, to calm down, but Knox wasn't listening, so Trevor let him be.

Knox could not stop muttering and Trevor tried to make sent of his muttering but found it difficult with Knox's thick Scottish accent that only got thicker as he muttered.

"Can't believe... damn idiot. So bloody blind; should've seen it earlier... before...I'm gonna kill that son of a bitch."

Knox muttered all the way to Babylon. His accent had gotten so heavy Trevor couldn't make out a single word anymore. Knox drove fast and hard, trying to make the four hour drive go by and to lessen his rage before getting to Babylon.

Knox managed to get to Babylon a little after ten that night. The little town was quiet as usual; not many people stayed out this late so the streets were bare.

"So this is Babylon?" Trevor had been told about the little town but had never been before.

"Yup, this is it. Not much of a town but its home." Knox had stopped muttering about an hour before they got to Babylon and was in control of himself again. Knox was able to fill Trevor in on what he had figured out once the muttering stopped but he was still trying to figure out what Knox was planning to do.

"Do you have a plan? Or are we just going to bust in and hope for the best." Trevor wanted Knox to think about what their next move should be, have things laid out so fewer things would go wrong.

"Not sure yet" Knox said. He had no idea what he was going to do, all he knew was by the end of the night he would have Gabriella back one way or another.

"Well what if we go to the police. I mean we have more than enough evidence now, proof that she was taken and you know where she is. They can go in and get her?" Trevor thought that it was better for everyone if the police did it.

"You don't know the local police here. They're useless due to nothing ever happening in Babylon. Once we know Gabriella is actually there, we'll call them." Knox pulled the car over across from a small house. Knox turned the engine off and looked across the street at the house.

The house was small and run down. No one had maintained it in so many years. The yard was overgrown; vines were starting to creep up the sides of the house. The front door was scratched up and the hinges were covered in rust.

"So that's the house?" Trevor wanted to know they had the right place, before they blindly broke in.

"Yup, that's the house." Knox kept his eyes on the house as he answered Trevor.

"And you're sure Gabs is in there?"

"She's in there alright. He's the only one who could have taken her." Trevor could hear the anger rise in Knox's voice again.

"Any idea how to get in?"

"Not sure yet, what if—" Trevor cut Knox off mid-sentence. To voice the idea that had jumped into his head.

"Why don't I go all the way around the house and see if any doors or windows are open, get a good lay out of the situation, while you stay here and keep a look out? Make sure no one comes?"

"Watch a lot of cop shows do ya?" Knox said sarcastically.

"Maybe, besides, everyone knows you need a look out when you're checking something out."

"Alright, go check out the house and I'll stay as a look out."

"Right" And Trevor hopped out of the car and snuck across the street over to the house.

Knox sat in the now quiet car, wondering how long Trevor would take. He wanted to go in and find Gabriella, hold her in his arms and know she was safe. Knox got bored quickly, sitting alone in the car so he searched his pockets for something to do.

Inside his jacket pocket, he found a letter from Gabriella, Faith had given him a couple of days before. He had forgotten all about it.

Knox looked out of the car to make sure no one was coming, that Trevor wasn't running back yet, and then he opened the envelope with his name on it and began to read:

My Dearest Aidan,

I know it has been a while since we've spoken and I hope all is well with you. As you know, the school year is almost over and that I am graduating from GreenBay this year. I do hope that you will join my aunt and uncle and come to the ceremony. I would particularly love it if you would be there, for there is someone I'd like you to meet. I doubt you'll like him at first but I know you will try and eventually will, if only because he is important to me.

His name is Trevor Beddingfeild and he's a psychotherapist. Trevor's also quite the musician; he plays piano beautifully and has a voice to match. We actually have a lot of fun playing together; we sound pretty good if I do say so myself. I like having someone to play with, I must admit. We even have our own song, if you can believe it; okay so it's one I wrote but still, it's ours.

It's actually somewhat cute the way it became our song. He had heard me playing it at the apartment one day and I guess he asked Faith about it and she gave him a copy. So he learnt my song, then during our, oh I think it must have been our eighth or ninth date anyways we were out for dinner discussing music and how we both played. In the middle of our conversation he busted out singing my song, in the restaurant; he was adorable. I think that was the moment I fell in love with him anyways I of course joined in on the second verse and we were the hit at the restaurant. It was our greatest date.

You know he reminds me a lot of you; he must love English just as much as we do, he has quite the passion for words, he's even writing his own book. He won't let me see a single page of course, so I couldn't tell you what it's about.

However, my real reason for writing you is to tell you that, well, I'm marrying him. I hope you will be okay with this one day. He makes me so happy it's hard to believe. I never imagined falling in love again after you. Never thought I could, but then I thought that the first time too, then you made me love. I'll always be grateful to you for that, for showing, teaching me true unconditional love. You, my dear Aidan, will always be my first and greatest love that will never change. I hope you remember that my love for you will never dwindle, and you will forever be in my heart. Please don't ever forget that.

All my love,
Yours,
Gabriella

Knox tucked the letter back into his jacket pocket and had to wipe a small tear from his eye. He understood Gabriella's wishes, but the letter had still shattered his heart. Knox had loved Gabriella with every fiber of his being and even though he still loved her, more than anything he had to do what was best for her. Knox had spent the last couple of days with Trevor and he knew he was a good man who loved Gabriella deeply. Knox knew she would be well taken care of.

Gabriella's safety and happiness was all Knox cared about. He would never forget their time together, and remember how precious and true their love had been. Knox resolved that once Gabriella was home and safe he would tell her it was okay, that he liked and thought Trevor was a good man. He would let her go.

As Knox made up his mind, he saw Trevor running back to the car so he quickly put himself together. As Trevor got back into the car, he started talking. "So all the doors and windows are locked but I think I saw an old cellar door in the back yard which I think will be our best way in." Trevor finished talking and Knox had this 'that was very professional' look on his face, but before he could say anything Trevor spoke again.

"I watch a lot of Bond. Gabs got me hooked." He shrugged his shoulders slightly and gave Knox a quick smile. "We should get going."

Knox nodded in agreement and they both stepped out of the car into the brisk night air.

They both took a side of the house; Knox took the right, while Trevor took the left. They were trying to be quiet as they made their way to the back yard. The front of the house was locked up as Trevor had said; Knox peeked through the living room window to check things out for himself.

Trevor was curious of what Knox was doing and came over to make sure everything was all right. They didn't see anything useful, just a messy living room; pizza boxes on the coffee table, empty beer cans and bottles strewn around the room. They couldn't see much more of the inside of the house; the smallest amount of kitchen, which looked just as messy as the living room.

A man walked in to the living room and Knox and Trevor dropped down into the bushes under the window so that they wouldn't be seen.

"Was that-?" Trevor asked very quietly.

"Yeah, it was." Knox's accent got a bit thicker again. Seeing him made Knox's anger rise. They quickly raised their heads to see if he was still there then they quickly moved out of the bushes and moved to the back yard.

The back yard was a junkyard. Old rusted cars; some were in pieces. The shed was more like a tree. Wooden walls, with the front side open with a workbench. Knox waited and watched as Trevor looked for the cellar door again, until something caught his ear; coming from the window, just at the bottom of the house.

It took Trevor a minute to find what he was looking for. Knox noticed Trevor hovering around a bush by the left side of the house.

"Trevor, what are you doing?" Knox asked Trevor quietly.

"Can't you hear it?" Trevor was still trying to find the other side of the bush, to the house.

"Hear what? I don't hear anything." Knox moved over to where Trevor was and tried to hear what Trevor could. Trevor stopped rustling the bush in order for Knox to hear. It was faint but it was there.

'I can see the sadness in your eyes
I can feel the pain within your soul'

"Gabriella." Knox said a bit louder than he had planned to, "I knew she was here. I knew it!" Knox looked over at Trevor and saw him smiling.

"What?" Knox wanted to know what Trevor was thinking that would make him smile.

"Oh, she's singing our song. It was the first song we ever sang together. She wrote it, and well… it became our song." Trevor stopped talking, he could tell by the look on Knox's face he had shared too much.

"Right, well we know where she is now, so all we have to do is get into the basement." Knox felt like he was talking to himself. Trevor had knelt down on the ground trying to get through the bush again, starting to get annoyed with Trevor.

"There's a window behind this damn thing, that's how we can hear Gabs' singing, maybe it's open?"

Knox bent down to help Trevor push the plant out of the way, sure enough there was a window with a piece missing; It looked as if a small ball crashed through it at some point in time. Trevor peered in the window but couldn't see much.

"It's too dark to see anything down—oh wait." A small light turned on so Trevor could see a bit more. Knox managed to find a spot where he could see what was happening. They hovered outside the basement window and watched, still trying to figure out how to get inside.

Chapter Twenty-Seven: Consequences

The basement door opened and the hallway light filled the dark basement. Gabriella's fear rose, she knew what was coming. Gabriella had grown to hate her captive. She dreaded each step he took down the squeaky staircase, because that meant he was that much closer to her. She had taken to singing whenever he came down into the basement. Singing calmed her and annoyed him.

> 'Cause we're all broken
> Our souls are in two
> We're all broken
> But we pulled thorough
> Yeah we're all broken,
> But I'll keep loving you
> Will you love me too?'

Gabriella's voice was shaky as she sang, but it brought her peace.

"Oh stop that singing already. All you do is sing, give it up." His voice was harsh and cold, and though he had once loved to hear Gabriella's voice, now it was full of pain and fear. He had not been able to find enjoyment in her voice since taking her. Every time he would tell her to stop singing, she would sing louder.

> 'You try and hide all that you are

Hoping no one will see you
You've seen some demons in your time, yeah
Well honey so have I, Oh'

He reached Gabriella and struck her hard across the face to stop her from singing.

"You know if you'd simply do as I say then I wouldn't have to hurt you." He reached out where he had struck Gabriella and began to stroke her cheek. As he stroked her red cheek, he leaned down towards her ear and whispered, "I don't take pleasure in hurting you." Then he kissed her cheek, then her lips.

Gabriella cringed as he kissed her. She hated his touch and he didn't stop after one kiss. He started to move down her neck when a loud thud came from outside. Frustrated he stopped what he was doing and the pair of them turned their attention to the window just about them.

He saw something quickly move away from the window, but couldn't catch what it was. He moved closer to the window, leaving Gabriella's side. She was chained to a bed, tears starting to fall down her bruised cheeks, hopeful that someone had finally found her, but fearful of what her captor might do to them should they fail to save her.

"David please, please, please David, stop this already, please." Gabriella struggled to get her words out. David glanced over at her, and then headed back up the stairs to find out who was outside.

As soon as the basement door shut, the window smashed in. The glass breaking startled Gabriella, but she knew better than to scream. Screaming would only hurry David's return. Gabriella looked up towards the window to see who was breaking in.

"Gabs, Gabs, you alright?" It was Trevor; he was trying to get through the window.

"Trevor, Trevor is that really you?" Gabriella surprised by Trevor's presence. "How'd you find me?" So many questions were forming in Gabriella's mind. She knew her questions could wait until after Trevor had gotten her out.

"Yeah, that's a really long story love." Trevor had managed to fit through the widow but he misjudged the distance and fell on to the cement floor with a *'thud'*. Gabriella gave a slight fright and frantically asked him if he was all right. Trevor assured Gabriella that he was fine as he got up and dusted himself off. Before Trevor did anything else he moved, over to where Gabriella was chained up he kissed her deeply.

"Oh God, I've missed you. " Trevor kissed her forehead and cheeks; he was so grateful to be holding his Gabriella again.

"I take it that was you outside making all that racket?" She said as Trevor started to figure out how to get her out of the chains David had placed her in.

"Oh yeah, well after we saw David hit you then make a move we well... fell against the window in outrage." Trevor was still trying to pull the chains apart.

"We? Who's we?"

"Oh, right, sorry. Knox, he's here too." Trevor was starting to get frustrated with the chains Gabriella was bound in.

"Knox, Aidan's here? But how? I don't understand. You two are here? Together? But..." Gabriella was beyond confused at this point, and trying to make sense of it all when Trevor spoke again.

"Yeah, like I said, long story." He said as he pulled against the chains again.

"Okay, that's clearly not working Hun." Gabriella stated, in hopes it would stop Trevor from pulling her wrists apart in the process of trying to rip the chains.

Trevor let go, realizing he was hurting Gabriella. "Okay, maybe there's something down here I can use." Trevor stood up and started to look around the dark basement. Just as he got up to move around the basement, the door opened with David and Knox thudding down the staircase.

Knox was walking in front with David behind him holding the back of Knox's neck in one hand and a tire iron in the other. As they came down the stairs Trevor and Gabriella could see Knox holding the right side of his head, as blood trickled over his hand from where David hit him.

"Well, well, who's this then? It seems you have two men trying to save you." David asked once Knox and he were standing in front of Trevor and Gabriella.

"So, is he another one of yours Gabs? Like Knox here and Kenneth." David's jealousy flooded his face. His grip on Knox tightened.

Gabriella was shaking her head, terrified by what might happen next. She knew David was blind to all reason. "I told you David, Kenneth and I were only friends—"

David cut her off, "Friends, right... like you and Knox were 'just friends' come on, don't give me that. I saw you and Kenneth together! Talking, laughing! I saw the way he would graze your arm, so don't give me the friend speech again. You don't know how to be 'friends' with a teacher." David had gone off and from the feel of things; this was an argument David and Gabriella had had many times.

"Is that why you took her? Because you thought she was seeing another teacher?" Knox said as he got out of David's grasp. The bleeding from Knox's head wound had started to slow and he was able to get some of his strength back.

"She shouldn't be with anyone but me. I'm the only one who truly loves her." David was now trying to justify his actions.

Trevor was having a hard time believing what he was hearing.

"You think she should be with you; the guy who took and tortured her for weeks on end. Are... are you out of your bloody mind?" Trevor wasn't planning to jump in, but his anger got the better of him.

"Seriously who the hell are you?" David was as angry as Trevor was and you could hear it in his tone.

"He's my fiancé David." Gabriella couldn't sit quiet any longer. Even knowing how David would react to the news.

"He's... your... what?" David struggled to get the words out. It wasn't what he was expecting to hear.

"Fiancé, I'm marrying him. I told you I wasn't involved with Kenneth." Gabriella was tired and hoped that if David understood then maybe she could go home. She doubted this would happen.

"I guess you lost her too, Eh Knox?" David wasn't sure of anything anymore. "He's still too old for you, why... why can't it... why not...?"

"You mean why not you?" Gabriella cut in; she could see the hurt in David's eyes.

Everyone went silent. David was unsure of his next move and the other two were hoping he would release Gabriella and let them leave. Knox was the first to break the silence.

"Come on David, it's over, we know you're the one who kidnapped Gabs and the police are already on their way to take you in. I called them from the car before you found me, so come on, it's over."

As Knox went silent, they all could hear the faint sound of sirens getting closer. David knew it was over and he had to make his mind up quickly on what to do. David started to shake his head mad and frustrated. This was not going how he thought it would. He made up his mind. David swung the tire iron he was still holding and hit Gabriella hard on the side of the head.

She lay unconscious on the bed.

David went in for another hit, but both Knox and Trevor went for the iron to stop him. The tire iron got knocked out of David's hands and all three men went down, trying to grab it.

Once David realized the tire-iron was too far away from his grasp, he started throwing punches wherever he could, not caring who he hit.

Gabriella was starting to come too turning on her side, her focus was coming in and out, and blood was falling down the side of her face where she was hit with the tire iron. She could barely make out all the fighting going on around her.

The three men were back on their feet, the tire iron forgotten on the floor. David got a good hit on Trevor, causing him to fall back, knocking into the old stand up freezer. Trevor knocked into it and the door fell open causing the body of Kenneth Madson to fall on Trevor. Trevor shouted, startled, getting the attention of everyone else in the room.

Gabriella screamed as Knox ran over to Trevor to help him get the body off him. David couldn't take Gabriella's screaming so he moved and picked up the tire iron that was just off to the side and headed towards Gabriella to shut her up. Knox had gotten Trevor out from under Kenneth's body and saw David walking towards Gabriella.

The police sirens were getting louder but David looked as though he was about to kill Gabriella and Knox knew there was little time left, he ran to intercept David but got there too late.

David hit Gabriella again, causing her screaming to stop and as David went for another blow, Knox got in the middle of it and the tire iron cut into his abdomen. David, in shock, let go of the tire iron as Knox fell back on to the bed, holding his wound. Gabriella struggled against the chains and finally came free. She moved around a knelt in front of Knox.

Knox was going into shock. His wound was bleeding out quickly and he was starting to feel light-headed, his vision getting blurry.

"No... no! No, please, no!" Knox could hear Gabriella saying, "No! You can't! Please..."

David, frozen in his place and Trevor watched Knox and Gabriella as the police sirens got louder and louder. They sounded as if they were right outside.

"It's okay love... it's okay." Knox said weakly to Gabriella as he reached to touch her face with one of his bloody hands. Knox had gone white in a matter of seconds and he knew this was the end. "I found you, it's okay." Every breath Knox took hurt and it was getting harder and harder.

Gabriella had tears falling from her eyes as she pressed her hand against Knox's cheek.

"You can't die, please no, you can't! I love you." Tears were falling from Gabriella's bruised, puffy eyes. She was losing the first man she had ever loved and the pain was too much.

"I love you too love. I will always love you." It was getting harder for Knox to speak. Gabriella leaned in and kissed him.

Knox's hand dropped from Gabriella's cheek and he was gone.

Chapter Twenty-Eight: Love

Gabriella felt as though she was trapped in a horrible nightmare; her head bleeding profusely while tears ran down her beaten, swollen, pale face. Lightheadedness was starting to set in as she held her first love in her arms while loud banging noises surrounding her. She could hear the world around her but felt like it was all so far away from where she was. People were running around her but her head hurt too much to focus on anything anymore. Then she heard a familiar voice.

"I think she's coming to; Gabs honey?" Gabriella could hear her Aunt Enid's voice as she fought to open her eyes. Once Gabriella's eyes were fully open she saw a room full of people: her aunt and uncle, Dr. Wiseman and Trevor. Trevor had a black eye and his right arm was in a sling from where he had hit the freezer. He looked badly bruised but was smiling Gabriella also saw a doctor and a nurse standing beside her bed.

"Where... where am I?" Everything was still a bit hazy and Gabriella was struggling to form her words.

"I'm Dr. Wills and you're in the hospital. You gave us all quite a scare, and that was quite the head wound, can you tell me your name please?"

It took Gabriella a few seconds before she answered him.

"Um it's... Gabriella... Harris." Her voice was still shaky and she was very unsure about everything.

"Good." Dr. Wills weaved around the room and sat on the edge of the bed as Gabriella sat up a bit. He grabbed his small flashlight out of his doctor's coat and shined it in both of her eyes, one at a time, checking her pupils.

"How to do you feel Gabriella? You've had some excitement these last couple of weeks." Dr. Wills had a soft smile on his slightly chubby face.

"Um... my head hurts and I'm really tired and sore." Gabriella didn't even try to smile back at the doctor. She was too tired to do much of anything.

"Yes, I'd imagine you would be. Well you haven't seemed to suffer any mortal damages. You're awake and talking, all very good signs. I think you will be all right my dear. I'd try to get some more sleep if you could, but in the meantime, you have some visitors. Are you up for it?"

Gabriella nodded her head slightly as she replied, "It's okay, and I'd like to see them." Dr. Wills nodded and moved off the bed to allow everyone else to see her.

Once Dr. Wills had moved aside, Gabriella noticed the two detectives' who had come in. Gabriella could guess what they wanted to talk about so she gently pushed herself up a bit more in her bed so she was almost sitting right up, and directed her attention to the detectives.

"Aidan?" was all she said to them, as her eyes filled with tears, hoping it was all a bad dream.

The older of the two detectives took a step in and replied.

"We're very sorry Miss Harris, he did not make it." His voice was course from years of smoking, but full of sincerity for the young woman he was addressing. While his partner stood quiet. She was young and looked unsure of everything, like she was fresh out of her uniform.

Gabriella shut her eyes, hoping that would slow her tears as she remembered the events that lead her here, and she remembered Knox.

Everyone in her hospital room remained silent as Gabriella remembered her first love. Once Gabriella opened her eyes and wiped her tears, she looked back to the detectives and gave him the okay to ask his questions.

Gabriella's aunt and uncle realized the detective was going to question her so they quietly left the room with Dr. Wiseman following behind them. They were happy to have their niece back but they were not ready to hear what happened.

Trevor moved standing next to Gabriella's bedside and took her hand, unwilling to leave her side.

The detective kept his place grabbed a small note pad out of his inner coat pocket and a pen ready to ask his questions.

"Can you tell me what happened to Kenneth Madson, Miss Harris?"

"Gabriella shook her head up and down.

"Yes, David beat him to death. Then in a panic he emptied the large freezer and put Kenneth in it." Gabriella had tears falling down her face again as she spoke about her friend.

The detective was nodding his head as he wrote down everything Gabriella told him. "And what can you tell me about David Thompson?" He asked.

Gabriella closed her eyes and more tears fell; she shook her head as she remembered the last couple of weeks locked in the basement, forced upon for David's pleasure, beaten time after time. "I... I can't... I'm sorry, I just—" The detective could see Gabriella wasn't ready to talk about her ordeal.

"It's alright, there's plenty of time for all of that." The detective was sympathetic to her situation and knew it didn't actually matter if she ever spoke about it. They had their man with all the evidence they could need. The detective moved to leave the hospital room with his partner when Gabriella asked him one last question.

"Detective..." he turned back to face her.

"Yes Miss Harris?" He asked.

"What... um... what happened to David?"

Even after everything Gabriella couldn't help but care, they had a lot of history; he had been her first friend and in her way, she always loved him. She wasn't willing to let go of their past just because he tried to destroy their future.

"Well, he's in our custody at the moment. We have a psychotherapist who is going to examine him, get a grasp on his mental state. But it looks as if he might get off with temporary insanity and he will be sent to Ridgefield Mental Institution." The detective wished Gabriella a good recovery; turned and left the room with his partner right behind him.

Gabriella gave Trevor's hand a squeeze as she turned to look at his bruised face with a slight smile on her swollen lips.

"What?" He asked sharing her smile.

"He's joining my father in the institution."

"So?"

"Well it's kind of funny. The two men I should have been able to trust with my life, both try to harm me, and then end up in the same mental institution." She would have laughed if she wasn't in so much pain.

"It's not funny." Trevor said even though he was smiling and as he thought about it more, saw the ironic humor in it all.

Dr. Wiseman, Enid, and John came back in the room, noticing the detective's had left. Gabriella admired all the faces that surrounded her. Her aunt Enid was still crying, so glad to have her niece back while Gabriella's uncle John held his wife, smiling as well, happy to have his family whole again.

Dr. Wiseman smiled at Gabriella and told her how glad he was that she was home, safe, and then took his leave, knowing she would talk to him when she was ready. Gabriella nodded goodbye to him then he was gone just like the two detectives.

Gabriella realized that the only person missing was Knox, and it broke her heart all over again. She squeezed Trevor's hand again as he sat down on the side of her bed. He gave a squeeze back; he knew she would need time and knew she would grieve Knox for a while, and that he would too. They had only known each other for a few days but in the end, he had quite a lot of respect for the man who saved Gabriella's life, a sacrifice he would never forget.

Gabriella stared into Trevor's bruised eyes; he had come for her.

"How long have I been in here?" Gabriella decided she wanted some of the blanks filled in. John ended up answering her.

"About a week, you slept for most of it. A couple of times you opened your eyes, but you were unresponsive." As John spoke, Gabriella noticed how tired he was. She imagined he had been worried sick about her, on top of taking care of Enid. He probably had had little time for himself.

"You gave us all quite the scare Gabs." Enid couldn't stop crying; John looked over at her and decided he'd better take her home.

"I'm going to take your aunt home for the night and we'll be back in the morning." John had a small smile on his face as he took the hand of his weeping wife and said Goodnight.

Gabriella turned back to Trevor who was admiring her.

"Do you know when I can go home?" She asked him. She never did like hospitals very much.

"In a couple of days, the Doctor's just wants to be sure you're okay before they release you."

Gabriella was nodding her head again.

"Okay, hey, are you ever going to tell me how you found me?"

"It was Knox. He showed up in GreenBay looking for you. He sought me out for help and then we didn't quit until we found you. We even went to Ridgefield to make sure your father hadn't taken you." Gabriella had to cut in when she heard that.

"You went to see my father, really?" There was surprise in her voice.

"Yes, we had to be sure and once you're better we'll talk about how you've been seeing him without telling me."

They both grinned at each other than Trevor went back to telling the story.

"Anyways, Knox had been receiving notes from David telling him to stop looking, once he recognized the handwriting we drove straight to get you." Trevor finished and kissed Gabriella on the forehead.

"Yes, but how did you know where in the house I was. I could've been anywhere." Gabriella wanted the whole story.

"Oh, that... well I heard you singing our song and I followed your voice." Trevor smiled again this time, feeling proud of himself.

"My knight in shining amour!" Gabriella said with a smile and a yawn. She was still exhausted from the past few weeks. Trevor shifted, letting go of Gabriella's hand, making her think he was leaving.

"Stay." She said tiredly.

"I'm not going anywhere." Trevor shifted the two of them so that they were lying in the small hospital bed together. Trevor started to sing their song softly and Gabriella started to drift back into sleep.

Gabriella was released from the hospital a few days later. Trevor had told her where Knox's grave was. They had buried him a couple of days after finding Gabriella, as he had no family there was no official funeral.

When Gabriella was released the detective gave her the possessions he had on him which included her last letter to him.

Gabriella knelt down in front of the tomb stating:

> *'Aidan Edgar Knox*
> *Beloved Friend,*
> *Beloved Teacher,*
> *Who will be deeply missed.'*

Gabriella found out that Trevor had paid for the tombstone. After everything Knox had done Trevor thought it was the least he could do. Gabriella laid flowers against Knox's tombstone as her eyes began to tear up. Holding her last letter to Knox in her hands, she spoke softly to the grave.

"I guess I never got to thank you. You never gave up on me, ever and there is not a day that will go by where I won't remember all that you've done for me. You saved me from myself you know. All those years ago, you saved me from being nothing more than a shadow in the world. I will always love you... I'm glad you got to meet Trevor before... we've agreed that our first son will be named after you... Knox... I think it will make a lovely name." Gabriella could hear faint footsteps coming up behind her and knew that Trevor was on his way.

Tears were falling down her rosy cheeks; she kissed the letter in her hands then placed it down next to the flowers.

"I love you," she whispered, as she stood up from the cold grass. "I'll be back soon."

Gabriella turned from the grave to see Trevor standing waiting for her just a few feet away. She took a last glance at Knox's final resting place then headed over to her fiancé ready to start anew.

CPSIA information can be obtained
at www.ICGtesting.com
Printed in the USA
LVOW12s1036020418
571948LV00001B/2/P

9 781773 028262